"Don't touch it. There may be fingerprints."

"I doubt it," Katerina said. "I think I felt gloves, not bare skin."

He lifted the folded paper with two fingers at a corner and laid it on a bare spot atop the dresser, then used a pencil to carefully unfold it. He stepped back and watched her reaction as she scanned the note.

"'Turn over the stash and we'll leave you alone'?" she read aloud. "What's that supposed to mean? I don't know anything about any stash. Do they mean drugs?"

"Your guess is better than mine," Max countered. "What do you think?"

She threw up her hands and began to pace. "How should I know? I don't have a clue."

"I wish I could believe you."

"Yeah," Katerina said, scowling at the piece of paper, "I wish you could, too."

CLASSIFIED K-9 UNIT:
These lawmen solve the toughest cases with the help of their brave canine partners

Guardian–Terri Reed, April 2017
Sheriff–Laura Scott, May 2017
Special Agent–Valerie Hansen, June 2017
Bounty Hunter–Lynette Eason, July 2017
Bodyguard–Shirlee McCoy, August 2017
Tracker–Lenora Worth, September 2017
Classified K-9 Unit Christmas–Terri Reed and Lenora Worth, December 2017

Valerie Hansen was thirty when she awoke to the presence of the Lord in her life and turned to Jesus. She now lives in a renovated farmhouse in the breathtakingly beautiful Ozark Mountains of Arkansas and is privileged to share her personal faith by telling the stories of her heart for Love Inspired. Life doesn't get much better than that!

Books by Valerie Hansen

Love Inspired Suspense

Classified K-9 Unit

Special Agent

The Defenders

Nightwatch
Threat of Darkness
Standing Guard
A Trace of Memory
Small Town Justice

Love Inspired Historical

Frontier Courtship
Wilderness Courtship
High Plains Bride
The Doctor's Newfound Family
Rescuing the Heiress
Her Cherokee Groom

Visit the Author Profile page at Harlequin.com for more titles.

SPECIAL AGENT

VALERIE HANSEN

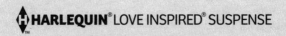
HARLEQUIN® LOVE INSPIRED® SUSPENSE

Special thanks and acknowledgment are given to Valerie Hansen
for her contribution to the Classified K-9 Unit miniseries.

Recycling programs
for this product may
not exist in your area.

LOVE INSPIRED BOOKS

ISBN-13: 978-0-373-67827-3

Special Agent

Copyright © 2017 by Harlequin Books S.A.

www.Harlequin.com

Printed in U.S.A.

For You have delivered my soul from death,
my eyes from tears, and my feet from falling.
—Psalms 116:8

Many thanks to fellow series authors
Terri Reed, Laura Scott, Lynette Eason,
Shirlee McCoy and Lenora Worth—plus editor Emily Rodmell,
who keeps us all on track.

And to my Joe, who is with me in spirit.
He always will be.

ONE

FBI agent Max West squared his shoulders and forced himself to walk away from the latest scene of destruction.

His job there was done. Unfortunately, the Dupree family crime syndicate, at least what was left of it, seemed determined to keep him and his team scrambling by randomly setting off bombs. Opal, his K-9 explosives detection partner, worked very well but it was frustrating to be called in after the fact.

He paused in the shade of an enormous oak and phoned Dylan O'Leary, the team's computer guru, on his cell. "I'm done with this one. Just the usual leftover components and a lot of jumpy people." Max sighed. "At least there was no loss of life *this* time. That family caught in the blast zone on the last one nearly made me turn in my badge."

"So, what now?" Dylan asked. "You thinking of leaving Northern California and heading home to Billings?"

"Maybe soon. I thought I'd look into the backgrounds of some of the Dupree underlings we've scooped up while I'm in the neighborhood. See if we missed anything on the first sweep."

"Little fish in a big pond," Dylan reminded him. "We got Reginald Dupree, the real brains behind the drug operation."

Max nodded. "While his uncle Angus kidnapped one of our best men and escaped. Has there been any word on Agent Morrow's whereabouts?"

"Sorry. No."

"Okay." Max opened the rear door to his black SUV to air it out before letting his brown-and-white Boxer, Opal, get in. "I checked our files last night and was on my way to the Garwood Horse Ranch when I got diverted to this call. Vern Kowalski, one of the Dupree drug runners, had ties there. When we arrested him he insisted he was working alone but it won't hurt to check. I can use a break and so can Opal."

"You're the boss, *Boss*."

Max barely chuckled. Being SAC, special agent in charge, of the Classified K-9 Unit was no picnic. A lot of responsibility rested on his shoulders, responsibility that weighed heavily. Yes, he considered this job his calling, but that didn't mean he never felt the pain of loss, never wished he'd been more successful and had prevented every explosion, every injury. Every death.

Closing his eyes for a moment he reminded himself that he was just a man, giving his all in terrible situations. Then he loaded his dog, climbed behind the wheel and continued his interrupted trip to the nearby ranch.

Katerina Garwood was halfway between one of the stables and the house, heading for her old suite, when she saw an imposing black vehicle pass beneath the ornate wrought iron arch at the foot of the drive. Unexpected company was all she needed. If her father came outside to see who it was and caught her trespassing on his precious property he'd be furious. Well, so be it. There was no way she could run and hide in time to avoid encountering the new arrival—and perhaps her irate dad, as well.

Chin high, she paused in the wide, hard-packed drive and shaded her eyes. The SUV reminded her of one that had assisted the county sheriff on the worst day of her life. The day when all her dreams of a happy future had gone up in flames.

Darkly tinted windows kept her from getting a good look at the driver until he stopped, opened his door and stepped partway out. Prepared to tell him to head up to the house if he needed to speak to someone in charge, she took one look and was momentarily speechless. The blond, blue-eyed man was so imposing and had such a powerful presence he sent her usually normal reactions whirling. When he spoke, his deep voice magnified those unsettling feelings.

"Katerina Garwood?"

"Do I know you?"

"No, but I know you. I'm Special Agent West. I'd like to talk to you about Vern Kowalski."

"I have nothing to say." She started to turn away.

"This is not a social call, Ms. Garwood." He flashed a badge and blocked her path. "I suggest you reconsider."

"FBI? You have to be kidding. I am so unexceptional that until recently people hardly noticed me."

"They do now, I take it."

She blushed and rolled her eyes. "Oh, yeah."

"Then you'll understand why I need to speak with you."

A quick glance toward the house told her she and the hunky agent had not yet been noticed. That was too good to last. As soon as one of the hands or the foreman, Heath McCabe, spotted her, word would get to her father and he'd be on the rampage again.

"Not here. Not now. We can meet in South Fork

later. I work at the Miner's Grub diner, on Main, near where the American River forks."

He quirked a brow. "What's wrong, Ms. Garwood? You seem nervous."

"It's personal."

"Everything is when you get right down to it." He reached for her arm as a familiar white pickup truck pulling a matching horse trailer rounded the nearest of three identical, rectangular stables and came to a stop.

She jerked free. Backed away. Her sky-blue eyes had widened and she was trembling. "I have to go. Now."

"Care to tell me why?" Max's gaze was unwavering. "Perhaps you'd better come with me and wait in the car while I have my K-9 partner check this place."

"What? No. I'm not going anywhere with you. I haven't broken any laws. All I did was believe Vern's lies and fall in love with him. It's not my fault I was duped. And I don't know anything about his secret life as a crook, okay? Despite all the nasty rumors, I'm a good person."

"Then why are you so jumpy?" Max continued to crowd her until she was ready to literally shove him away.

Unable to help herself, Katerina darted glances back and forth between the immense house and the complex of stables where the foreman had stopped with the horse trailer. Was he on the phone to her dad already? There was no way to tell. And no way to avoid another terrible scene once Bertrand was notified.

There was only one sensible course of action. She had to plead her case in person, and to do that she had to reach Heath McCabe despite the determined agent. Staring into the distance on his opposite side, she used that momentary distraction to slip away.

Max was on her in a flash, grasping her arms and holding fast. Katerina began to thrash around. If her father saw her now he'd be even more positive she was worthless. Tears of frustration filled her eyes.

I will not cry, she insisted to herself. *I'm through letting any man make me cry.* Nevertheless, a few drops escaped and trickled down her flushed cheeks.

Suddenly, she was pulled free. The middle-aged foreman had come to her rescue. His arm was drawn back, ready to deliver a punch, and the agent's hand was reaching for his sidearm.

Katerina intervened. "Stop!" She gestured at McCabe. "This is just a misunderstanding. I wanted to keep you from telling Dad I'm here and Agent… West? Agent West must have thought I was running away."

The adrenaline in her system had bolstered

Katerina's courage and she faced him as boldly as she could while her insides quaked.

Max met her gaze head-on. "Your father? Why didn't you just say so?"

"I did. You weren't listening."

"No, you were acting guilty, behaving like a scared kid trying to make a run for it."

"I'm not a child. I'm twenty-two."

"I know. I read your file."

She was thunderstruck. "There's a *file* on me? An FBI file?"

"Yes, of course."

"Why am I not surprised?" She felt the starch go out of her like a sigh lost on the wind. Her concentration moved to the foreman. "Please don't tell Dad I'm here and make him mad all over again. It was bad enough when he threw me out the first time because of my horrible love life. I just want to pick up a few of the personal things I left behind."

McCabe doffed his cowboy hat. "I'd never do you that way, Miss Katerina. You know I wouldn't." He gestured back at the truck and trailer. "If I didn't have to get these horses to the vet for checkups I'd stay here and help."

"Do you have Moonlight with you? I looked for her in the stables when I got here and she wasn't in her usual stall. That whole section was empty."

"Your horse is safe and sound with me." The

wiry foreman eyed Max. "All right if I leave or are you plannin' to shoot me?"

"I just came to talk to Ms. Garwood. If she had explained the reasons for her reluctance in the beginning we'd probably be done already."

"You gonna be okay if I go, ma'am?"

Katerina smiled. "The horses come first with me. You know that. I'll be fine." She noticed both men staring at the house across the driveway. "If Dad catches me here and starts yelling again I'll just do what I did before. I'll leave."

"Okay, then. You and this cop goin' into the house now?"

She looked to Max for confirmation.

"I do need to speak to Bertrand Garwood. If that's a problem for Ms. Garwood I see no reason to confront her father while she's present. She and I can talk out here."

"Now there's a good idea," Katerina said. "You can go, Heath. Take good care of Moonlight and the others."

"Yes, ma'am."

Watching him drive off, Katerina turned to Max. "All right. If you want to ask me questions let's get it over with. There's nothing I can tell you that I haven't already told the local police and the agents who arrested Vern, but I suppose it won't kill me to go over it again." She made a face. "I learned a hard lesson."

"Oh? Did you?"

Her grimace grew and her eyebrows arched. "Yes, Mr. Agent, I found out that my loving father will disown me and throw me out if I make a mistake. I also learned to never trust a glib-talking man, and that includes you."

She would have been happier if he hadn't seemed to find that final statement amusing.

"Let's sit in my car," Max said, gesturing with his arm. "After you."

"Can't I go get my clothes and stuff first? It took a lot of courage for me to drive back out here and as long as Dad hasn't noticed me yet, I'd like to finish what I came for."

"I take it you expect me to just hang around while you do as you please."

"Why not? I'm no criminal."

The unwavering look she was giving him as she spoke demonstrated determination. And she was right. Law enforcement had nothing on her, personally. He'd merely hoped that some small fact she didn't even think was important would point the way to more of the Dupree associates, perhaps even to herself, although at this juncture he viewed the young woman as more of a pawn in a crooked chess game than a true player.

Blowing out a breath, he conceded. "Okay. Do you want any help?"

"No. The less noise I make, the less likely I'll be noticed. It's a big house and when my father works on his accounts he always shuts the den door."

"All right. I'll wait in the car."

As soon as she started toward the garden leading to the nearest door of the ranch-style home, Max turned back to his SUV. There was something appealing about Katerina Garwood; something he couldn't quite put his finger on. She was far too young for him, of course. It was too bad she hadn't been born ten years earlier.

Max's thirty-three wasn't exactly ancient but there were times when he felt like Methuselah, particularly when he and his team failed to prevent mayhem.

Movement at the edge of his peripheral vision snapped him around. *Now* what was she up to?

"Hey, where do you think you're going?" he called.

Turning to walk backward, Katerina waved. "I left some empty boxes in my truck. I'll be right back."

"Sure, you will," Max muttered. He wasn't taking any chances that she'd try to flee so he fired up his SUV, made a U-turn and headed for the main gate to block it. If worse came to worst and she got away from him he could always call for backup, but it would sure be embarrassing.

* * *

Katerina paused to watch his maneuvers. The man was paranoid. What did he think she was going to do, try to outrun his powerful vehicle in her little ol' pickup truck? Talk about David and Goliath.

"Yes, but David won," she mused, happy to have been reminded of a Bible story where the seemingly weaker combatant triumphed in spite of everything.

Before she had time to pivot and continue on her previous path toward the stable, an intense light flashed.

She instinctively ducked and covered her head with her arms.

Her eardrums felt as if she had plunged to the depths of the sea. Debris hit her as the blast concussion sent her—and pieces of one of the barns—flying.

Landing on the hard-packed dirt with the realization that a building had exploded, her last conscious thought was for the well-being of her favorite mare, and others. "Thank You, God. Moonlight is safe with Heath."

Max's heart was in his throat. Nothing in the files had suggested that Katerina was involved in the recent rash of bombings, nor had there been any threats against the ranch. Not that he knew of, anyway.

He was running toward her as he called 9-1-1, identified himself and reported the explosion. "At the Garwood Ranch. That's right. Between South Fork and Groveland. Send an ambulance and the fire department. I see a lot of smoke."

Dropping the phone on the littered ground beside Katerina he fell to his knees and began to check her over. "Lie still. Don't move. An ambulance is on the way."

She moaned and shifted position.

Max held her shoulders gently but firmly. "I said don't move. You could have broken bones or spinal damage." He could tell by the way her eyelids fluttered that she was only half-conscious. That was the worst time for exacerbating injuries. Out cold she wouldn't move. Conscious, she'd probably try to do as she was told.

People were running to evacuate frantic horses from the remaining, undamaged barns. Dogs circled and barked, adding to the mayhem. A heavyset man stomped across the dirt drive. He was wearing boots, a Western shirt and hat, and jeans belted with the biggest gold buckle Max had ever seen.

"Who are you?" the man bellowed.

"Max West, FBI. You must be Bertrand Garwood."

"Smart man. What're you doing on my ranch?"

He pointed at the prone figure of his daughter. "And what is *she* doing here?"

The coldness of the older man almost gave Max the shivers. No wonder Katerina didn't want to face him. Well, *he* wasn't backing down. Although he couldn't safely release her until paramedics arrived he looked up and glared. "Your daughter is unconscious, Mr. Garwood. I'm not certain how bad her injuries may be. I don't see any bleeding other than a split lip so she may have escaped the worst of the blast. It's too soon to tell for sure."

"Just get that trash out of here as soon as you can." He started to turn away. "I've got valuable livestock to see to."

If Max had not been busy tending to Katerina he might have resorted to language he hadn't been tempted to use in ages. What a pompous excuse for a parent Garwood was.

Max gazed down at the injured young woman and gently stroked strands of honey-blond hair off her forehead. There was a first aid kit in his car but he didn't dare leave her unattended to fetch it. Close by in the SUV, his trained K-9, Opal, was using her deep boxer bark to alert the world to danger, even though the worst of it was probably over.

As soon as the ambulance and fire department arrived, Max planned to assert authority and insist that he and his K-9 partner perform a bomb

sweep for additional devices. It was his job—
and Opal's—to ensure no one else got hurt without actually revealing the overarching mission. It
was going to be tricky to investigate Kowalski's
crimes without exhibiting too much interest in the
man's former connection to the Duprees.

He looked at Katerina again and realized he
didn't want to turn her over to the care of the EMTs.
He would, of course, because it was the right
thing to do, but he wasn't going to like relinquish-
ing control before he was certain she was okay.

TWO

Katerina could hardly breathe. Disoriented, she opened her eyes. The back of her head throbbed and her ribs refused to allow her to fully inhale. Gasping, she fought to regain her senses, to sort out confusing memories.

A weight was on both her shoulders, holding her down.

"Don't try to get up," someone ordered gruffly. "An ambulance is on its way."

Nevertheless, she tried to move.

"I said, hold still."

There was a gentleness underlying the otherwise firm tone and it gave her a sense that she was being well cared for. "Who? What?" Flashes of reality returned. "The stable! The horses!"

"They'd been taken out. Remember?"

"Only—only from the one barn."

"That's the one that blew."

"Oh." Blinking up at the face of her companion she saw mostly shadow. Sunlight behind him gave his short blondish hair a haloed look. The brightness kept her from reading his shadowed expression. She sank back down with a moan. "My head hurts."

"I'm not surprised. You hit the ground hard."

Her heart sped as she realized she could have been even closer to the barn when it disintegrated. What could have caused an accident like that? There was nothing more volatile than horse liniment kept near the animals. Even the tack room was safe.

The man restraining her shouted, "Medic! Over here. Everybody else stand clear."

"I'm all right. Really. I need to get out of here."

"The only place you're going, Ms. Garwood, is to the hospital."

"No. I don't have insurance. I can't afford to be hurt." She pushed against his hold momentarily, then sagged back.

Bright flashes of colored light sparkled behind her eyelids. Shooting pain banished any thought of trying to stand. Escape was unthinkable.

Katerina felt as if she were falling into a bottomless abyss. Fog surrounded her, bearing her ever deeper into unconsciousness. Longing for release, she ceased to fight it. Rational thought fled.

The world, and her troubles, faded away.

* * *

Max stayed on at the Garwood Ranch to assist local authorities in searching for additional devices in the unaffected outbuildings and house after Katerina had been stabilized and transported in the ambulance. From what he could deduce from the damage, the explosion in the stable had packed a lighter punch than the others he'd recently investigated. Unfortunately, an ensuing fire had wiped out much of the evidence and what the flames didn't consume, the firefighters' high pressure hoses had dispersed.

By now the place was swarming with law enforcement, fire personnel and crime scene investigators. He was relieved that he and his K-9 had not discovered more bombs because a crowd like that was hard to safeguard.

When he reported to the incident commander, a fire department battalion chief, he brought Opal with him. "My dog and I have completed our search. All clear."

"You sure?"

Max laid a hand gently on the boxer's head and stroked between her ears. "Opal is positive. That's good enough for me."

"Okay. Thanks. I can't believe you were already on scene when this happened. Is that some new FBI deduction technique that we haven't heard of?"

Max chuckled. "Not hardly. I was here to follow up with the Garwoods regarding another case my team is working. What can you tell me about Vern Kowalski?"

"Not much." The chief paused to radio instructions to an engine crew. "Pull down that west wall. I don't want to see a rekindle and lose another barn."

As soon as the man turned back to him Max asked, "Had you met Kowalski?"

"Briefly. The guy wanted to join our volunteers but he didn't make the cut. Katerina seemed to like him, though."

"I gathered, since she was going to marry him."

"Yeah. I hope she's gonna be okay. Nice girl. Her daddy's a real piece of work, though. He was hard to get along with before he got elected mayor of South Fork. Now he's impossible."

"Any word on her condition?" Max asked, remembering her attempt to avoid treatment and her father's unfeeling reaction to her condition. How could any parent see his child injured and just walk away?

"Not yet. We shipped her to the hospital in Mariposa. Paramedics said she could have a concussion. Hard to say without X-rays."

"What became of Garwood? I know he was

here for a while." Max made a sour face. "He's hard to ignore."

"Yeah. Sheriff Tate took him off the property in a patrol car. They're old buddies."

"I see. Then I'll talk to the Garwood I can find and head for Mariposa." Max scanned the scene. "Just make sure your people bag and tag as many clues as possible. I'll notify Quantico and have an agent pick up the evidence for processing."

The chief didn't look particularly pleased to share jurisdiction but didn't argue. Instead, he nodded and returned to the smoldering wreckage.

Max was pouring fresh water into Opal's bowl in the backseat as he checked in with Dylan at headquarters. "The ranch owner is AWOL at the moment so I'm going to follow up with the injured daughter, providing she's conscious."

"The one who was engaged to one of the men arrested in the Dupree sweep?"

"Yup. That's the one."

"Just watch your back," Dylan cautioned. "I don't care how idyllic it looks up there, you're in more danger than a gold prospector defending himself against claim-jumpers back in '49."

Max had to smile. "I have Opal and a cell phone and radio, and I'm armed. I'm covered."

"The dog will always work but don't count on electronics if you get down in some of those deep valleys. Besides, the Duprees play rough."

"I know. Thanks," he said, ending the call and drawing his fingers down the ridge of the old scar remaining on his left cheek as he recalled the events originally surrounding that injury five years before. Max knew that nobody lived forever, but he simply could not accept the premature death of a child on his watch. Worse, he had unknowingly contributed to that disaster by trusting the boy's father when the man vowed he'd cut all ties with the drug culture.

Clenching his jaw, he shoved aside the painful memory. If that senseless tragedy had taught him anything, it was to be far less gullible. No one had fooled him since, nor would they do so in the future. Criminal minds were devious in myriad ways. All he had to do was keep himself from accepting anything—or anybody—at face value without concrete proof of innocence.

Take the Garwoods, for example. The young woman he was on his way to see may have looked harmless but she was so unnaturally nervous he was having second thoughts about her. It was hard to attribute all that angst to a strained relationship with her father. Yes, the man was vindictive, but lots of people experienced difficult family situations without quaking in their boots. A more likely scenario was that Katerina knew about the bomb and had miscalculated the timing.

The worst kinds of criminals were the ones

who were able to fake innocence so well. Katerina might have fooled the firefighter he'd spoken with but Max would not be as naive. He had not risen to a command position on his team by letting himself be tricked by pretty faces or sweet smiles.

He didn't care if the whole world thought he was inflexible and opinionated. He did his job. And he never lost focus. Not anymore.

Katerina was exhausted. She'd been poked, prodded, x-rayed and scanned. All she wanted to do at the moment was sleep despite the nurses who kept coming into her room and waking her to check her vitals.

The door to the hospital room made a swooshing sound as it opened. She squeezed her eyes shut against the bright overhead lighting. "I'm awake. Please let me rest."

The ceiling-mounted curtain was pulled to isolate her bed. Someone's latex-covered hand clamped hard over her mouth and she tasted fresh blood from the cut on her lip. Tightening her muscles sent pulses of pain shooting through Katerina's battered back. She tore at the glove and tried to see who was attacking her but a ski mask covered his features. A harshly whispered warning came next, "Stop fighting." She tried. Panic argued against it. All she could manage was to hold a little more still after he planted a heavy arm across her chest.

"Don't scream."

Although she managed a weak nod she was not agreeing. This was a busy hospital. If she could manage to shout, even once, help was bound to arrive. Hopefully, it would be enough for a rescue.

The gloved hand eased its pressure. The arm lifted. Trembling, Katerina froze and stared at the figure hovering over her bed. He seemed tall, although it was hard to tell for sure when she was lying down. What she could see of his bare arms beyond the short sleeves of the faded green scrub outfit he wore told her he was tanned but not unusually so. If she'd been able to see his hands they would have given her a better idea of whether he worked inside or on a ranch or farm.

Should she speak at all? she wondered. If he was planning to kill her, surely he wouldn't have awakened her first. But why bother her at all? Why was any of this happening? She gritted her teeth in frustration.

"Vern sent me," the man gritted out.

Anger mingled with her fear. So that was it. "Why?"

He didn't answer. She could see the rapid blinking of his eyes through the holes in the mask as he swiveled his head nervously. Finally, he reached for the IV needle taped to her arm and started to pull it out. "It's too dangerous for me here. You and I are leaving."

Katerina pushed his hand away, took a deep breath and screamed, "No. Help!" at the top of her lungs.

Her attacker jumped away as if he'd been shot with a Taser. At that moment she wished she had one to make it real.

He lunged to cover her mouth once more, but she evaded him by rolling to the side. "Help me!"

The physical pressure lifted. Katerina continued to shriek with primal fear, no longer articulate.

A hand touched her shoulder. Voices mingled.

When she turned her head there were two nurses at her bedside, one blond, one graying and motherly looking.

Katerina peered past them. "Where did he go?"

"Who, dear?"

"The man. He had a mask on and he—"

"You've been through a severe trauma," the blond nurse interjected. "We can't give you a stronger sedative just yet, because of your head injury, but the doctor said we could take the edge off your pain. You may be having a delayed reaction to what happened to you or to the IV meds. I'll report it to him."

"I am not hallucinating," Katerina insisted hoarsely. "There was a strange man right here in this room. He threatened me." She lost hope when she saw the nurses exchange knowing glances.

"All right. Just lie back and rest," the motherly one said, patting Katerina's hand. "I'm sure you'll be released soon. In the meantime, one of us will be close by. Use your call button if you need anything."

"You're not even going to look for the guy, are you?"

"As I said, we'll report your symptoms to your physician, dear."

Meaning, they still thought she'd been hallucinating or dreaming. Was it possible? *No*, she concluded. A trick of her brain would not have made her cracked lip bleed again. There had been a man's hand pressed over her mouth. And he'd intended to take her away with him.

Vern was in jail. So who had accosted her?

Max knocked before entering Katerina's room accompanied by a nurse. He'd expected to see her in bed but had not anticipated the reaction he got. She took one look at him, fisted her sheet and gathered it up under her chin like a shield. Her skin was pale, her mouth slightly swollen and her eyes reddened and puffy as if she'd been crying.

He hesitated, raw emotion churning through him. despite outward calm "The staff says you've been having a rough time, Ms. Garwood. Do you remember who I am?"

"FBI. You were there when the barn exploded."

"Right. I looked after you until the ambulance arrived. How are you feeling?" he asked gently. "Are you up to finishing our conversation?"

As he watched, Katerina tried to raise herself into a sitting position and blanched. She looked ill beyond her injuries. Max beat the nurse to her bedside and steadied her. "Easy."

With the weight of her shoulders resting on his arm, Katerina sighed. "Sorry. I forgot myself for a second. It's been a rough day."

Max stepped back as the nurse raised the head of her bed slightly, and then he asked, "Better now? Or do you need a few more minutes?"

"I'll be fine as long as I don't try to move too quickly." She eyed the young nurse in the background. "Would it be possible for us to talk alone?"

Max nodded. "I see no problem with that. Leave the door ajar on your way out, please," he told the nurse. As soon as she had left he took out a small digital recorder, clicked it on and renewed his interest in the patient. "What can you tell me about the incident at the ranch this morning?"

"Me? You were there, too. I don't know any more about it than you do. One minute I was yelling back at you and the next thing I knew I was knocked off my feet." Her voice softened a notch. "Thanks for looking after me."

"You're welcome. Now think. Did you see or hear anything unusual earlier?"

Her brow furrowed. "No. I wasn't actually there for very long. I'd just stopped by to pick up the last of my clothes and things. I told you that."

"I understand you no longer live there."

"No. I don't. My father was so angry when Vern was arrested for smuggling and distributing drugs he blamed me for ruining the family reputation and threw me out."

Max struck a pseudo-relaxed pose. "And you're surprised by that? It was pretty risky to keep company with a lowlife like Kowalski in the first place. You must have suspected he'd eventually be caught."

"I had no idea he was a crook."

That he didn't believe for a second. "You were supposed to be marrying the man. How could you possibly not have known?"

"Because he was slick and because I was naive, I guess." Her cheeks warmed visibly and his chest constricted when he saw moisture glistening behind her lashes. But he reminded himself he had a job to do. "Look," Katerina went on, "I'm not stupid. I actually have a pretty decent IQ. But Vern wasn't like the other men I'd met. He said all the right things at the right times and I fell for him. How was I to know he was using my father's horse business as a cover to distribute drugs?"

"Intuition? Didn't Kowalski ever say or do anything that made you suspicious before he was arrested?"

"No." She broke eye contact. "Later."

Aha! Now they were finally making progress. "When?"

"Promise you won't look at me like I'm a horse short of a full team?"

"Yes. Go on, Ms. Garwood."

"When I had a scare earlier this afternoon, the nurses said I imagined everything and blamed it on my injury and pain medicine."

Leaning closer, Max listened carefully. "Is that what you think?"

"No. Well, maybe. I know I was terrified. I was drifting in and out of consciousness when somebody clamped a hand over my mouth and told me not to struggle."

"Here?" Every instinct in him was on alert. "They told me you'd been having nightmares but what you claim is highly unlikely."

"I know," Katerina agreed. "The nurses who came after I shouted for help insisted I'd been dreaming. I've started thinking they may be right. It's just that my lip bled and hurt more afterward and I can't see any other reason for that much physical change, not even my screaming when I got so scared."

"Describe your assailant."

She huffed. "Pick up any mystery novel and

you'll know. Ski mask, hospital clothes and gloves. No prints, no ID, no nothing. He wasn't as tall as you are and not as muscular, but…"

"Okay. What makes you think he had anything to do with Kowalski?"

"Because he told me Vern sent him," Katerina said haltingly. "I—I thought he was going to kidnap me. That's when I started yelling."

Max gave her the kind of stern, menacing look he usually reserved for perps he was grilling. "You didn't want to go with a friend of your fiancé?"

He saw her fists clench. "No."

"Because he scared you?"

Despite the obvious discomfort of pushing herself up with her elbows, she met his severe gaze with one of her own. "No," she almost shouted before lowering her voice, her throat raw. "Because I am an honest person and I want nothing to do with criminals, their friends or their disgusting business. When is everybody going to get that straight?"

The glistening of her unshed tears was more convincing than her insistence. Either she was a great actress or she was truly upset.

Max stood and backed away to make a call. He arranged to have the police check recent activity on the security cameras monitoring the halls and place a guard outside Katerina's room for the night. Then he returned to her. "When you're released from here I'll come back and drive you home. Then, if you're up to it, I'd like to take you back to the ranch and walk you through exactly what you did before I arrived." He handed her a business card after jotting his private cell number on it. "Call me when you're ready to go."

"What if I refuse to take orders from you and arrange my own ride?"

"I don't advise it."

Katerina nodded. "I'll call, but not because you're scowling at me. And not because I'm guilty of anything and hope to fool you. I'll call because you believe there really was a stranger in my room when everybody else insists I'm crazy."

THREE

In retrospect, Katerina was not keen on asking the taciturn federal agent for a ride home the following day. The problem was, she had few other options. Her poor pickup truck was probably toast after the barn blew up and except for a few friends who worked in town and maybe the ranch foreman, there was nobody she felt she could call. Heath McCabe would be in deep trouble with her dad if she asked him, so she did the sensible thing and dialed Max West's private number.

"West."

"Um, hi. It's Katerina Garwood. They've discharged me and I need a ride if your offer is still open."

"Of course. Did you have a quiet night?"

"As quiet as it gets in a hospital," she said with a wry smile.

"Understood. I can be there in twenty. Does that work?"

"Yes, I think I'll last that long. I'd walk down to the cafeteria for a latte if I wasn't still a little dizzy."

"Are you sure you're okay to leave?"

It was refreshing to hear genuine concern reflected in his question. "The doctor says I am so I'm going. This is not a fun place. I want out."

"Hang tight. I'm on my way."

She wanted to tell him how truly thankful she was that he'd made himself available but did not. Her instinct to trust had been so ravaged by Vern's betrayal and her father's rejection she couldn't rely on her instincts. Not yet. Besides, considering all she'd learned about law enforcement in the past few months, Max was probably only being nice to her in order to catch whoever had menaced her or set the bomb at the ranch. Or because he still had doubts about her innocence. Given his job and her background, she figured the agent would become even more suspicious if she acted overly friendly.

Katerina let her thoughts wander as she perched on the edge of the bed in the too-big green scrub outfit the nurses had provided. Her own clothes were ruined. The back of the shirt she'd been wearing looked as if it had been blasted with a shotgun, as her tender shoulder blades kept reminding her. Jeans were tougher but hers were so dirty she'd refused to put them on. Her leather cowboy boots were about the only thing she could still wear, although they slipped without thick socks.

"I should fix my hair," she muttered, wondering why it mattered when she wasn't meeting anyone but Agent West. Nevertheless, she slid off the bed, took a second to steady herself, then made her way to the bathroom mirror. Nurses had helped her shower and the hospital had provided a comb but her long, wavy hair resisted efforts to tame it. Pulling on tangles made her scalp hurt unless she carefully held each portion, so the job took a while and was less than perfect. Well, too bad. If her volunteer taxi driver didn't approve, so what?

That hostile attitude not only struck her as wrong, it made her blush. Whatever his motives, Max was no chauffeur. He was going out of his way to be nice to her. The least she could do was try to look presentable.

A knock on the door startled her. She steadied her balance on the sink and called, "Come in."

One look at him today, when she was fully lucid and aware, took her breath away. Not only was he tall and ruggedly handsome, his dark blue uniform shirt fit the way it should, displaying a powerful form with broad shoulders and a narrow waist, unlike many men his age. How old was he? she wondered. It was impossible to tell, although her best guess put him somewhere in his early thirties. Definitely not over-the-hill. Far from it.

Max acknowledged her with a brief nod. "Ready?"

"Absolutely." She began to move toward him, hiking up her sagging scrubs as the pants started to slip.

He eyed her. "Nice outfit."

"The boots are mine. The rest is borrowed."

He cleared his throat but Katerina still heard the chuckle he was trying to mask when he said, "Glad they had your size."

"I could fit two of me and a couple of the ranch dogs in here at the same time," she quipped, stopping and spreading her arms to better display the two-piece scrub ensemble. That was an error. The room started to tilt and she made a grab for the doorjamb. "Whoa."

Beside her in a fraction of a second, Max caught her around the waist. "Easy. You sure you're ready to leave?"

"I'm signed out and everything. Just had my chickens scattered, as Mom used to say."

"Your parents are divorced?" He was guiding her toward the open door.

"No. My mother passed away when I was fourteen. That's when I started putting all my efforts into training horses."

"So, last year?"

Katerina knew he was teasing to try to lift her spirits and played along. "I'm twenty-two, going on forty, which my file should tell you." Leaning on his big, strong arm as they walked, she asked, "How about you?"

Max gave her a wry smile. "Older than dirt."

"That old, huh?"

Pausing at the doorway he looked back. "Do you have anything to take with you? Meds or bandages or anything?"

"Just that plastic sack of ruined clothing at the foot of the bed. Since I'm on a tight budget I need to try to salvage the jeans."

Making sure she was well balanced, he fetched the bag and picked up where they'd left off. They were almost to the exit when a nurse spotted them and tsk-tsked. "You're supposed to leave in a wheelchair, ma'am. We don't want you falling."

"As you can see I'm in good hands," Katerina said, smiling and leaning her head toward her stalwart companion, genuinely glad he was by her side.

It wasn't until they left the hospital and she saw his formidable black SUV that she sobered. Lighthearted moments aside, there was big trouble in the little towns in and around historic gold country. First there had been the drug busts and now somebody was setting off bombs. Other incidents had been reported on the local news so she knew her family ranch was not the only target. The question was, did somebody destroy the barn as retribution for her former ties to Vern? It was certainly possible, and terribly disconcerting.

She remained silent as Max helped her into the SUV. Above all, she wanted him to find the perpetrator and put him in jail.

And not blame an innocent bystander. Like her.

"So, where do you live?" Max asked casually.

She arched an eyebrow. "You mean you don't already know? That's not very comforting."

"Okay, I know," he said with a smile, flicking a brief glance across the seat at her. "I figured you might have a shortcut or better way to get there. These winding roads are hard on Opal."

"Who?"

"My K-9 partner. She usually rides closer to me but I put her in her portable kennel box in the back when I have a passenger. You'd have met her if you hadn't been knocked unconscious."

"Oh, I love dogs! Is she a German shepherd?"

"No. And don't you dare laugh. She's a boxer."

"A *what*?"

"You heard me. I get teased almost everywhere we go. She's really great at detecting bombs but people are more used to seeing breeds with longer noses."

"No kidding. Why in the world would they train

a boxer for that? I mean, they can't have as keen a sense of smell with such a short muzzle."

"You'd be surprised."

"I'd like to meet her. Dogs and horses were my best friends while I was growing up. There's a darling black lab at the ranch that I'd adopt in a heartbeat if Dad would let me." She hesitated, seeming sad. "So, tell me more about your dog. How old is she and how long have you had her?"

"She's about four. My team has begun rescuing at least one pup for every mission we go on and we don't rule out any capable canine, purebred or mutt. Opal's a good example of hidden talent. She showed aptitude for detecting explosives and hearing or smelling electronics such as detonators, et cetera, so she was trained and assigned to work with me." He cleared his throat before continuing. "We're not master and dog, we're partners. We both have badges. I just happen to be the only one with a driver's license and a gun."

Katerina chuckled quietly. "That's comforting." Pointing to an upcoming turn, she said, "May as well take 49 and double back a little. My place is between here and the ranch."

"I'm surprised you didn't ask more about the horses in that burning barn." He was surreptitiously watching her expression and most likely wondering if he would find out more than she intended to reveal.

"Heath had Moonlight and her stablemates in the trailer, remember?"

"Yeah. Handy."

"What was?"

"That that barn was totally empty when the bomb went off."

"You don't think Heath was responsible, do you? I mean, he's been with the family since he was a teenager. I trust him like an uncle."

He hardened his jaw. "What about your father? Could he have needed insurance settlement money?"

"Of course not. Don't be ridiculous."

"Then you realize who that leaves." His gaze was telling, as it was meant to be.

"Me? No way. I'd never endanger people or animals. How many times do I have to say it? I am one of the good guys."

"Until I believe it." Another sidelong glance caught her evident consternation.

"I don't care if you believe me or not, Mr. Big Important Government Agent, except that you're wasting time. Instead of harassing me you should be out looking for whoever is really behind the bombing, not to mention the lowlife who tried to grab me from the hospital."

"I'm keeping my eyes open," he vowed soberly.

"It's not your eyes I'm worried about," Katerina countered, "it's your closed mind." She turned her face to the window and added, "'There is none so blind as he who will not see.'"

Max knew she was quoting scripture, although he couldn't recall exactly where in the Bible that phrase was found. He didn't mind her doing that. What bothered him was the slim possibility she might be right.

Katerina's apartment was a tiny space above a boarded-up, vacant storefront on a side street in South Fork. It had been all she could find when she'd been ousted by her father and, although she was now employed, anything else was still beyond her budget. If she hadn't worked at a diner, eating might have been, too. Not that she wanted anyone to know. The way she looked at it, as long as she had a roof over her head and enough to eat, she was blessed.

If the K-9 cop/agent was surprised by the appearance of her current dwelling in contrast to the posh Garwood Ranch he hid it well. That pleased her. She'd already had so-called friends from her ranch days turn up their noses at her efforts to make a home out of a veritable hovel. This handsome man with his perfectly pressed uniform and gleaming car never batted an eye.

"I'll get Opal." He eyed her scrubs and smiled. "That shade of green sure isn't your color."

Katerina returned his grin. "Oh, I don't know. It matches my skin whenever I move too fast and get dizzy."

He was chuckling to himself as he opened the hatchback and released his dog. Katerina waited to see what a boxer in uniform looked like. Since the idea was ludicrous she assumed the image would be, too. Opal, however, jumped down on command and stood at the ready, a picture of the perfect canine standing at attention as if she were a seasoned soldier ready to do battle.

"Can I pet her?" Katerina asked. "I don't want to mess up her training."

"Glad you asked. When our dogs are wearing their vests or special harnesses like this it's best to keep your distance. I'll let you play with her later. Okay?"

"Okay. She really is beautiful and impressive. I'm sorry I made fun of her breed." Katerina continued to smile, only this time she was focused on the dog. "Please convey my sincere apologies?"

"Opal never holds a grudge," Max said with a slight smirk. "I think you'll enjoy watching her work. She's intense when she's on the trail of dangerous substances."

"Wonderful. Well…" She eyed the building. "I'll go on up and change before we go back to look at the ranch. That was what you wanted to do, right?"

"Right. After Opal and I have scoped out your apartment."

It was hard for Katerina to stifle an unladylike snort. "I don't think there's much danger of anybody even finding this place, let alone wanting to blow it up. It will probably fall down on its own soon enough."

"Still, we should go with you. Opal can always use the practice and there's no lead on whoever was in your hospital room yesterday."

Reminded of this, Katerina was willing to let him accompany her. After her recent close calls she was unsteady in more ways than one. Her nerves were firing like kernels of popcorn in a pan of hot oil and she didn't like the feeling one bit.

"Okay. I have an outside stairway in the rear. That way I don't have to bother opening the old hardware store to get in."

"It looks unique." Max squinted to peer through the dusty windows. "I almost expect a prospector to step out carrying a pickax and a gold pan."

"You aren't far wrong. The date over the doorway says the building goes back to the mid-1800s. I suspect it was expanded as needed during the gold rush." She paused when she reached the base of the wooden stairway in the rear. "Single file from here. Be my guest."

Max hesitated and raked her with a solemn stare. "If I didn't have Opal to alert me, I might wonder if you wanted me to go first because you already knew it was dangerous."

"Oh, for…" Katerina pushed past him and stomped up the stairs in her loose boots. The door wasn't locked. Almost nobody in South Fork locked their homes. She straight-armed the door and barged in. One gasp and she skidded to a halt.

Max caught up. "What's wrong?"

"Look! It's awful!"

He took one peek and agreed. "Wow. I take it you're usually a neater housekeeper than this."

"Well, duh." Katerina rolled her eyes cynically. "I never tear the stuffing out of my only chair just for fun. And I don't have a pet tiger, so those slashes must have been made with a knife."

He drew Opal closer with the leash and placed his other palm on the grip of his sidearm. "Wait here."

He didn't have to tell Katerina twice. Her boots felt nailed to the floor. Trembling, she watched the dog put its nose to the carpet and lead the handsome agent toward her bedroom. Was it simply searching for a scent or had it picked up the odor of an explosive? What if there was another bomb? What if it went off? She shivered involuntarily. The old hardware store was rickety at best and there was no telling what kind of combustibles might be stored below. She had never wondered before. Now she wished she'd been more paranoid.

Taut nerves insisted she not linger despite the agent's orders to the contrary. Checking to see if he was visible and not seeing him or his dog, she began to sidle out the open door. One step. Two…

Max's shout of "Hey!" startled her and she thought he was yelling at her until he added, "Federal agent. Freeze."

Katerina tensed. A darkly clad figure came barreling toward her. There was no time to move before the onrushing man lowered a shoulder and smashed into her like a quarterback trying to make a touchdown. She spun. Fell. Heard more shouting and sensed someone jumping over her prone figure.

Wood cracked. Splintered. The outside railing gave way. A dog yipped. *Opal!*

Katerina flipped over and scrambled for footing. Her head was pounding. Her vision blurry. Unsure, she blinked rapidly, astounded.

Max was hanging from the remains of the broken railing by one hand while his canine partner clung to the partially collapsed stairway edge, legs splayed and claws digging in.

The moment Katerina peered over at him he shouted, "Get the dog!"

It never occurred to her to argue or hesitate. Only after she had hold of Opal's harness and was hauling her to safety did she wonder why she hadn't been bitten. As soon as the K-9 was out of the way, the agent swung a foot onto the edge of the step Opal had vacated and pulled himself up.

All three sat there, catching their breaths. Only the dog seemed unperturbed.

"Thanks," Max said. "You okay?"

Katerina began to nod, then thought better of it. "Just peachy. I have a pounding headache, the whole county thinks I'm a crook, somebody is out to make an even bigger mess of my life than it already is, my ex sent a thug after me and we all could have been killed just now, even poor Opal. Otherwise, I guess I'm fine."

"You *guess*?" His tone was gruff.

"Hey, don't snap at me. I just saved your partner."

"Did you get a look at the guy? Was it the same man as at the hospital? All I saw was a black hoodie and jeans."

"I have no idea," Katerina insisted. "He rushed me so fast I hardly knew what was happening. Where was he hiding?"

"Beats me. Must have been in the kitchen. He wasn't in the living room or bedroom." Standing, he reached for her hand. "Come on. You need to go in and see if anything's missing. Since he was still here, I assume he didn't find whatever he was looking for, but you should take a look."

"I'm not going to like what I see, am I?" she asked warily as he pulled her to her feet.

"No, you're not. Watch your step."

Max kept hold of her hand as he led her back into the apartment. Opal followed, no longer acting concerned or even interested. That was a relief. Katerina was actually feeling pretty good until she saw her bedroom. Or what was left of it.

Max was impressed by this young woman's inner strength. Most would have wept over the mess the thieves had made. Someone had destroyed her thin mattress down to the box springs, then torn the covering off it, too. There was no way she was going to be able to sleep there until replacements were found, and even then it wouldn't be safe with the only easy exit missing part of its railing.

"We should leave the evidence as is until a crime scene team can look it over," he said. "I'm not sure how much of your clothing is usable anyway."

"It better be okay. I can't afford to buy new."

"I'm sure your father—"

"Don't even go there," she snapped. "My dad made it very clear that he wanted nothing more to do with me. I am not asking him for a thing."

"Then how about appealing to your fiancé's friends? I'm sure they have plenty of money." Max hated to keep needling her but necessity and training insisted. All he'd need were a few new names and the investigation could head in a fresh direction. Making a seemingly nice young woman spitting mad was a small price to pay considering what he eventually hoped to get out of her.

During the course of most investigations he had no qualms about stirring up volatile emotions. In Katerina's case, however, he found the method personally objectionable. Necessary, but distasteful.

The fire in her gaze and stubborn set of her jaw told him he might have hit the bull's-eye. Instead of telling him off, however, she merely went to the dresser, stuffed a few things into a pillowcase and walked stiffly past him to the door.

"I've reported this incident," Max said. "You can't leave until the police get here."

Katerina wheeled. One hand was clenched around the opening to the pillowcase and the other was fisted at her side. "I'll be in the car."

"Fine. And while you wait, think. What are they looking for? And who blew up the stable? Nobody becomes the focus of continuing attacks without reason. You must have a good idea who's doing this, and the sooner you tell me, the sooner I'll go away."

Her nostrils flared, her cheeks turned red and

she glared at him. "Maybe the same criminals did it all."

"As a profiler, I find that highly unlikely, Ms. Garwood. Whoever set the bomb in the barn couldn't have been looking for something you'd hidden there because they'd have taken a chance of losing it forever in an explosion and fire. This apartment, however, was ransacked but not destroyed. That tells me they didn't find what they were searching for."

"They'll be back?" She chewed her lower lip. "Of course they will." Color drained from her face, leaving her so pale Max worried she might be ready to keel over. There was only one thing to do. He phoned Dylan and briefed him, then asked, "Can you get me another room at that hotel where I'm staying? I need a place to put Ms. Garwood, at least for one night."

Dylan's response wasn't as positive as Max had anticipated but the young woman's wide-eyed astonishment helped him decide on an alternative. "All right. Do what you can. If I have to, I'll give her my room and Opal and I will crash in the car. It won't be the first time."

Meeting Katerina's gaze, he was startled to see unshed tears and even more surprised when she said, "You'd do that for me? When you still blame me for the bombing?"

"Let's just say you're a person of interest. Dylan

will wrangle another room. Don't worry. He always comes through for the team."

A tear slipped silently down her cheek. She brushed it away. "You're not nearly as tough and mean as you pretend to be, are you, Special Agent West?"

His "No comment" brought a soft laugh from her that reminded him of joy-filled times he'd thought he'd forgotten, times when life had seemed easy.

A few moments of looking into her eyes was almost more than Max's heart could take. He turned away. If an impartial observer had accused him of emotionally closing down he would not have argued.

Katerina Garwood was as dangerous to his mental and emotional stability as the deadliest of criminals. The only thing that would save him was that he knew it.

FOUR

"I hope you're going to tell me that your agency is picking up the tab for both hotel rooms," Katerina said as Max concluded his business with the police and joined her with Opal. "Because if not, I'm going to be the one sleeping in the car."

"Don't worry about it."

She rolled her eyes. "How can I not worry? I've been living from paycheck to paycheck and hoping for good tips ever since the ranch was raided and Vern was arrested. I'd expected my life to change but not the way it has."

"Can't you get a training job at another ranch?"

"Not around here. Not with my undeserved reputation."

"Maybe your dad will mellow and invite you to come home?"

"Maybe. When it snows in Death Valley," Katerina countered. "I'm not holding my breath."

Max started the SUV. "The police don't think the burglar left any clues. Neither do I, but they collected possible clues anyway. Are you sure the guy in your hospital room mentioned Kowalski's name?"

"Yes. And no." Katerina pulled a face and slowly shook her head. "At the time it happened I was positive. The more I think about how implausible it sounds, the more I doubt myself. I'm sorry. I know it's hard for you to take anything I say at face value so it must be driving you crazy that I can't tell for sure. Believe me, it isn't easy being me right now."

"*That* I can buy," Max replied, with a twinkle in his eye. "I've made arrangements with a local sheriff's deputy to deliver more of your clothing to the hotel after they finish going over the apartment. It's the best I could do."

"Female deputy, I hope." Katerina felt her cheeks warming. "I guess I shouldn't be picky but I'd feel better if a woman did it."

"She's a she."

Katerina sighed and sagged back against the seat. "Good."

"While you're relaxing," the agent said, "Why not close your eyes and try to picture the hospital room incident. Take it slow and let's talk it through. You were sleeping and something woke you, right?"

"Uh-huh." Her sleep-heavy lids lowered. The motion of the vehicle began to lull her. "I remember thinking how the nurses kept coming in to check on me. I heard that whooshing sound of a door opening and sensed a presence."

"What did you see?"

"Nothing, at first. My eyes were closed. I told the person I was tired and wanted to be left alone." She shivered. "That was when he put a hand over my mouth and pressed so hard he made my lip bleed again."

"Could you have bumped it in your sleep, instead?"

"I had one arm strapped down with an IV and was lying on my back. It would be difficult to hit myself accidentally."

"Okay. Go on."

"I already told you the rest. The guy said Vern had sent him and wanted to talk to me." Sensing Max's attention, Katerina opened her eyes and looked toward him. He was scowling. "What?"

"That can't be right," Max said. "Kowalski's in jail. There's no way this so-called friend of his could have been taking you to him. Besides, why would he? All he'd have to do was tell you Vern wanted you to visit him."

Puzzled, she mirrored his expression of doubt. "You're right. Not that I want anything more to do with Vern or his buddies."

"Are you sure he mentioned your fiancé's name?"

"*Former* fiancé." She grimaced. "Why would

anybody pretend to be associated with a criminal? Do you suppose the man thought I was on the wrong side of the law, too?"

"He could have. That does seem to be the accepted opinion around here."

"Don't remind me. If I had the money I'd pack up and move away. Far away. I'm never going to escape my mistake otherwise."

"And what mistake would that be?"

Max's tone was even but the portent of his question chilled Katerina to the bone. "Falling in love, okay? I'm not talking about anything else and I really wish you and everybody else would quit gawking at me as if I were about to steal the family silver. I thought my dad was the worst offender until I met you, Agent West."

To her chagrin her companion quirked a smile. "Glad to be of service."

As he drove leisurely toward the historic hotel, Max made little further conversation. He wanted to grill his lovely passenger but decided to bide his time and let her fill the silence as most folks tended to do naturally. A lot of criminals were their own worst enemies in that regard. Either they couldn't help boasting or they got to rambling on about something inconsequential and their subconscious led them to reveal clues before they realized they were doing it.

He chanced a sidelong look at Katerina. Sleep seemed to have overcome her. Her eyes were closed and she appeared totally relaxed. Little wonder. Now that the adrenaline rush from encountering the fleeing prowler had worn off he was weary, too. If there had been a café or gas station along the narrow, winding country road, he would have suggested they stop for coffee.

Katerina stirred. Yawned. Stretched, then winced as her bruised muscles obviously objected. "Where are we?"

"GPS says we're halfway to the hotel. Is there any place along here to grab a decent bite to eat? I think we both need a break."

She studied the bright dash screen and pointed to a section of road. "There's a little hole-in-the-wall place there, in Fish Camp. Hard to know if they'll be open, though. It's more likely on weekends when long lines of tourists drive past on their way to Yosemite."

"I understand it's a pretty park."

"*Pretty?*" Katerina shifted sideways and stared at him. "It's amazing. You've never been there?"

"Nope. It was part of my briefing for this assignment but thankfully I've had no reason to go there on business."

"You never get a vacation?"

"I could if I wanted time off. It's not a top priority." He didn't have to be looking at her to interpret the sound of disgust she made.

"I don't believe it," Katerina huffed. "You face death on a daily basis, yet you don't take the time to smell the roses. What kind of life is that?"

"The kind I prefer," he replied, sobering and clenching the wheel more tightly. There had been a time when he'd had plans to start a family, to behave the way so-called normal people did. That idea had ended abruptly when a traffic accident had claimed his fiancée's life. Max had then thrown himself into his work and found the solace that otherwise escaped him. He saw no reason to rethink a lifestyle that had been working well for the past three years.

"Up there." Katerina distracted him by leaning forward and pointing toward his side of the road. "See the weathered red-and-white building? That's it."

Incredulous, he nevertheless slowed and signaled for a left turn. "It's still in business?"

"Last I heard. I don't get out here much these days. Which reminds me. You never said anything about my pickup. Is it totaled?"

"Probably. The local police had it towed into South Fork to clear the scene. I'll find out for you."

"Thanks. *Again.*" She pulled a face. "I'm getting sick of having to thank you for helping me when I know you have ulterior motives. I suppose, when you figure out I really am innocent, you'll hit the road and I'll never see you again."

"That is likely. My headquarters is in Billings, Montana."

"And you were sent clear down here? Weren't there any bomb-sniffing dogs in California?"

"I really can't discuss it."

"Can't, or won't?" she asked.

"Both. Let's just say it's classified and drop it, okay?"

Max was concentrating on his rearview mirror as he made the left turn. To his surprise, a battered old dump truck behind them turned and parked by the weathered building, too.

Katerina pressed him. "Well, what *can* you tell me?"

He chose to refrain from explaining his elite FBI unit but he did shrug and try to divert her attention. "Do you recognize that truck? I think it may be following us."

"What do you mean, following us? When did you notice it? Why didn't you tell me?"

"Don't panic. Most criminals prefer better, faster wheels so I doubt it's a problem." He saw her shade her eyes and squint at the rusty, dented truck. If its engine was as decrepit as the rest of it, they had nothing to worry about.

"I don't…" Katerina began before a sharp inhalation. "Oh, no."

"What? What is it?"

"Shadowed like that, the driver reminds me of the man in the hospital. Doesn't he look like the prowler we chased, too?"

"Maybe. There's one good way to find out. Stay here."

Max undid his seat belt and the safety on his holster with one fluid motion, then opened the door on his side and stepped out. Keeping the SUV between himself and the much larger truck, he pivoted toward it and studied the vehicle silently. If the other driver had ignored him he wouldn't have grown more apprehensive. However, instead of proceeding into the snack shop the way a normal traveler would, the man behind the wheel froze and returned Max's steady stare.

That was not a good sign. He started to circle the front of his own vehicle, intent on confronting the truck driver.

A second man occupied the passenger seat. Max rested his palm on the grip of his sidearm. No one spoke.

The engine of the old truck revved, proving that it was far from ancient. The hair at the nape of Max's neck prickled. Something was very wrong. If both men got out and rushed Katerina, could he protect her? He and Opal probably could, although he was loathe to endanger his K-9 partner unless it was absolutely necessary.

Max raised one hand, palm out and open. "Afternoon. Can I help you fellas?"

Neither man responded. Max reached for his badge. "Federal agent. Please keep your hands where I can see them and get out of the vehicle slowly. One at a time. Driver first."

Instead, the men ducked out of sight. Because the cab of the older truck sat so high off the ground, Max was no longer able to see them from where he stood. He started to draw his gun. The engine roared, drowning out his shouted order to stop. No officer of the law would discharge his weapon under those circumstances and apparently the men in the truck knew it. The driver backed into the road, quickly reversed and ground gears to start forward.

Max ran back to Katerina, slid behind the wheel and grabbed his radio to alert local police, then commanded, "Fasten your seat belt."

"We're not going to chase them, are we? I mean, how fast can they possibly go in that old truck? It's on its last legs."

"Don't be so sure. It sounds as if they have a new engine under their hood. Until reinforcements catch up to us we're going to keep them in sight. If they really are connected to Kowalski I don't want to lose them."

She braced herself as they took off in a squeal of rubber. "You think they *are*, don't you?"

"What I think is unimportant. It's what we discover after they're pulled over and searched that counts."

"I'd rather walk," Katerina yelled. "Let me out."

He couldn't, of course. If the men knew her by sight he'd be able to tell by observing their initial expressions when confronted. If they were merely unrelated lawbreakers he'd see that, too. Katerina had to be with him when the stop was made. This was too perfect a scenario to waste. Besides, if he let her out, she'd be vulnerable.

"We're staying together," Max yelled back at her. "It's safer."

"Doesn't look like it to me!"

Her blue eyes were wide, one hand fisted on the grip above the passenger door, the other grasping the edge of the seat. Yes, Katerina was fearful, but there was also a sense of wild adventure about her. Under different circumstances he might have guessed she was having the kind of fun a lot of folks experienced on a roller coaster.

Had their current situation not had the potential to turn deadly, Max might have chuckled out loud.

Whipped from side to side on tight, fast corners, Katerina kept her lips pressed together despite the awareness that a good, loud scream would feel wonderful.

Freeing.

Speaking of freedom, Max seemed to be gaining on the old truck. "I think we're catching them."

His "Yeah" didn't sound as upbeat as she'd expected.

"What's the problem? We don't want to lose sight of them, do we?"

"No. But I don't want to corner them all by myself, either. This isn't technically my jurisdiction and if the stop didn't go as planned, a lot of bureaucrats could end up twisting in the wind, me included."

"Is that what *special agent in charge* really means? You pay dearly for bad decisions?"

"In this case it may be. Hang on. They're slowing more."

"What are you going to do?"

"Without armed backup? If it were just me and Opal I'd order them out of their vehicle and hold them at gunpoint."

Katerina arched her eyebrows and made a face. "Hey, it's not my fault I'm still here. I told you to let me out and you refused."

"It was the right decision. It simply complicates things at the moment."

"Ya think?" She knew it was wrong to needle him but he'd been so convinced she was on the wrong side of the law that his current dilemma hit her as ironic. And amusing, provided the men in the big truck stayed away until reinforcements had time to arrive.

"Um, is it just my nerves or is the truck stopping?"

"Stopping. In the middle of the road, no less. The first car that takes that next corner too fast is liable to hit head-on."

She noted the hard set to the agent's jaw, the way his big, strong hands gripped the steering wheel. Clearly, he was having to make some crucial decisions and she hoped one of them included turning around and running for their lives.

Max eased his SUV to the far right of center and set the parking break. "You stay put. Lock yourself in. If anything happens to me, use the radio to call for help." He handed her the mic. "Push this button, talk, then release it so you can hear replies."

"Whoa. Where do you think you're going?"

"To order them out of the traffic lanes before they cause an accident."

"I thought we were waiting for backup."

"You are." Taking the mic momentarily he reported his position and plans to the county dispatcher, then stepped out and slammed the door.

"A fine mess this is," Katerina muttered. An answering whine from the rear of the SUV reminded her that Opal was back there. Releasing her seat belt, Katerina flipped onto her knees and shinnied between the backs of the front seats until she was within reach of the portable kennel box. Opal was not only drooling she was wagging her whole rear end.

"If I let you out will you promise to behave?" she asked the dog. "Your partner might need you and I could sure use the company."

Woof.

"That's what I thought. Okay. Here's your leash." She opened the kennel grate and grabbed the dog's harness. "Hold still, will you?"

The friendly canine's antics were enough to take Katerina's mind off the tenuous situation and bring a smile. "Yeah, Opal, I agree. He's the kind of guy to try riding a wild mustang with no saddle or bridle and then wonder how he ended up in a heap on the ground. I'm glad he's your partner, not mine."

Together, they returned to the front seat. Opal took the passenger's place so Katerina eased behind the wheel. The dash resembled an airplane cockpit with gauges she didn't recognize and equipment that looked like multiple radios, not to mention the computer system she'd seen Max use briefly.

Parked to the right rear of the bigger truck, Katerina could no longer see him. Neither could Opal, which clearly disturbed them both. The dog began pawing at the inside of the door.

"No, Opal. Your boss said for us to stay right here and that's what we're going to do unless…" *Unless I hear shots or something equally as bad*, she thought. Her hands rested naturally on the steering wheel and she sighed. "Why didn't I ask exactly what he meant when he told me to call for more help if he needed it. How am I supposed to know?"

Woof.

"My sentiments exactly." Katerina had always talked to animals and was reassured to have Opal beside her. "You're the one with the fancy training. So, what's the standard protocol for this situation?"

Instead of the silly, drooling look the dog had been exhibiting, she began to focus out the windshield and stare at the large truck. Katerina's focus followed Opal's. It almost looked as if the thing was moving. Backward. Toward them. There was little room to spare to the right before the ground fell away into a steep canyon!

A few native live oaks rose above the edge, their canopies giving the false impression that there was solid earth below. Pines, however, clearly demonstrated that they were rooted far below with only their tops visible.

What was the penalty for driving an FBI vehicle without permission? Katerina wondered. There was no time to ask and even less time left to decide. If they stayed where they were, that lumbering old truck could shove them off the road as if they were a child's toy. Either she took matters into her own hands and saved herself and Opal, or Max would be scraping them up at the bottom of the canyon. Looking at the problem that way made it easy to act.

Katerina dropped the idling SUV into reverse and wheeled it out of imminent danger by cutting the back bumper to her left. She was now back in the traffic lanes and could see oncoming cars slowing long before they got close to her. So far, so good. Now where was Max?

The heavy truck kept backing until one set of dual axels was balanced on the edge of the berm. Then it began to jockey sideways in the roadway, clearly intent on reversing directions despite the cramped space.

Katerina muttered a panicky prayer and gripped the wheel. She'd driven trucks pulling horse trailers and handled big vans at the ranch so she was pretty sure she could drive Max's SUV without wrecking it. Steering it down a winding mountain road backward fast enough to stay ahead of an oncoming truck, however, was another story.

Eyeing their surroundings, she looked for a way to slip past their adversary and escape uphill. It was impossible. The truck would soon be pointed straight at them and she'd have nowhere to go.

A wall of rock rose to her left at the edge of the pavement. A dropoff into a steep canyon lay to the right. She had lost her chance to mimic the huge truck and make a successful three-point turn before it took up the center of the road.

There was no room left for evasion. They were trapped.

FIVE

Max jumped back, gun in both hands, feet apart in a shooter's stance. "Stop!"

The dump truck kept inching along.

He raced to Katerina before the other vehicle could complete the last of its tight maneuvers, shoved her aside, slid behind the wheel and tromped on the gas. He was just in time.

With the SUV slewing backward he whipped the wheel hard then slammed on the brakes. They skidded in a circle that left blackened swirls of rubber on the road.

Katerina screamed.

Max straightened their trajectory and sped downhill. Ascending traffic was already backed up for quite a distance. All he could hope for at present was that the thugs in the disguised truck would continue to pursue him and ignore innocent civilians.

"Call this in," he ordered Katerina. "Tell them

what's happened and give the dispatcher our up-
dated position."

Although her hand was shaking as she reached
for the radio, he could tell she had control of herself. Except for that one piercing scream she
was actually responding to the crisis so well he
couldn't help but be impressed.

"Can't you go faster?" Katerina asked as soon
as she'd finished using the radio.

"Yes, but I don't want to lose him."

"Why not?"

"Because it doesn't matter who is doing the
chasing. We still need to know where these guys
are and being ahead of them is almost as good as
following."

"Says who?" She strained to see past Opal to
check their outside mirrors.

"Opal. Backseat. Go. Down," Max ordered. The
K-9 obeyed instantly.

Katerina took advantage of the space. "Thanks.
I wasn't sure if she'd let me move over."

"You shouldn't have opened her kennel."

"Sorry. I was afraid for Opal. If we'd been
pushed off the road she might have been trapped
inside the car. I wanted her to have the best chance
of survival."

He had to give credit where it was due. "That
was quick thinking when you backed up. Otherwise I might have had to shoot the truck driver."

"Would you have?"

"Not if there was any other option," Max said solemnly. "I don't suppose you'd like to tell me who you think is in the truck."

"How should I know?"

"Just asking." He continued to monitor the behemoth behind them and was satisfied it was still on their trail.

Ahead, as the road straightened and the countryside opened into valleys and pasture, cars were lined up behind a farmer's tractor and hay bailer in their lane. Max was not pleased. "Uh-oh." He flipped on his red lights and hit the siren, hoping to clear the way. Most of the passenger cars pulled over but the farmer seemed oblivious.

Max saw Katerina's feet brace against the floorboard. Her hands pushed forward to the edge of the dash. "Look out!"

He did the only thing he could since there was no room to pass; he slowed to a crawl. And braced to be hit from behind. "Hang on."

As far as Katerina was concerned, he couldn't have convinced her to let go if he'd tried. Every muscle in her body was taut, every nerve firing. This was scarier than her toughest dressage competition. At least when she was in the show ring she was in charge. Putting her life in this agent's hands was proving to be a poor decision despite his valiant efforts to protect her. Assuming they lived through the next few minutes she intended to thank him, despite the fact he kept giving the impression he thought this predicament was all her fault.

Then again, Katerina reasoned, her thoughts sizzling as they raced like a wildfire, if Max had believed her from the start, his choices might have been different and neither of them would be sitting here like a lame duck waiting to become roadkill.

Horns behind them started honking. Katerina peered into the side mirror. Her jaw gaped. "Where's the truck?"

Instead of answering, Max grabbed for the mic. "This is FBI Special Agent West again. Be advised, we're now southbound and stuck in traffic. Suspect vehicle has turned off on a farm road near mile marker 92, heading west and kicking up a dust cloud. If you have eyes in the sky you may spot the truck. Otherwise, we've lost him."

The radio crackled. "Copy. Do you still need backup?"

Katerina was astonished to hear him say, "Negative," before signing off.

"What do you mean, 'negative'?" She continued to watch the disappearing dust. "Are you just giving up?"

"We need to choose our battles. If those guys were who and what we thought they were, they'll be back. The secret is to stay alert and be ready for anything."

"Easy for you to say," Katerina grumbled. She plopped back in the seat. "What now?"

"We could make another stop." His gaze was less intimidating this time than she had expected. "Are you up for that visit to the scene of the explosion?"

Her wry sense of humor surfaced and helped her cope. "Garwood Ranch? Sure…why not. I was just almost shoved into oblivion on a winding mountain road. After that, how hard can it be to face my grumpy father?"

"On a scale of one to ten?"

She made a face at him. "Very funny."

"Hey, you started it. Would you rather check out the ranch tomorrow? With all our racing around we're actually not far from our hotel."

"Could we put it off?" She hated to give in to fatigue but the stress of the last couple of days had left her easily exhausted. She stifled a yawn.

"Sure. I have some files to look at and I imagine you and Opal could use a good night's sleep."

"Only if I get my own room," Katerina quipped. "I like your dog but I'm too tired to fight her for the bed the way I had to when we shared the front seat. She takes the space she wants and I get whatever is left over."

"She knows how important she is to me," Max said, smiling.

Katerina knew when she was bested and kept her thoughts to herself. Truth to tell, she would have gladly shared any space she had with Opal. At least the dog didn't make judgments about her character. The thing that made Max's actions so unbelievable was knowing that he still believed she was in league with the men who had influenced Vern, yet was willing to help and protect her. At times like this, Katerina actually wished she did know more about her former fiancé's illicit acts. If she'd paid more attention when they were together she might be able to aid law enforcement and be part of the solution instead of part of the problem.

Sighing, she relaxed against the seat and gazed out the window. Summer sun and California drought had browned most of the grass on the rolling hills. Fire danger was already extremely high, which was why the South Fork Founder's Day parade had been temporarily postponed, much to Mayor Garwood's chagrin. She hoped the predictions of upcoming storms would come to fruition and temper the danger despite the fact that she wouldn't be riding Moonlight in the parade for the first time in years.

Mulling over happier times, she had managed to let go of much of her earlier tension when Max asked, "Did you ever hear Kowalski mention the name Dupree?" which set her back on edge as if she had never calmed down.

"No. I read it in the newspaper but Vern never told me he knew them."

"This is a big state but you live in a small town. Surely you must have realized your boyfriend needed a job. What did you think he did?"

"Sold insurance," Katerina said with a frown. "When I asked why he didn't try to sell some to Dad, he said he never mixed business with pleasure." She made a face. "I should have guessed that his relationship with me was part of his *business*."

"What about his living arrangements? If you were still at home, where was Kowalski?"

"He had an apartment in Oakhurst. I thought he was spending his time at the ranch to be with me, not to use my family's transport vans to disperse drugs." She looked to Max for confirmation. "That's what the paper said he was doing. Is there more you're not telling me?"

"All I can say is that the Dupree organization is widespread and can be deadly. Details are classified." Max paused as if making a decision before continuing. "You probably read that we lost track of a member of our team, Jake Morrow."

"Oh, no." Katerina was truly sorry. "That's terrible. Did you find him?"

"Not yet. But we will."

"No wonder you're so determined."

"It's my job," Max countered. "I always do it to the best of my ability no matter what."

"I know," she said soberly. "I just wish I were able to help."

"Yeah." Max's jaw muscles clenched. "So do I."

The hotel named after Bret Harte was as quaint as any B and B in the gold country. Three stories of restored Victorian splendor were nestled in the shade of live oaks and buffered by steep hills to the west. In the canyon behind, where brush and trees had not masked the long-ago activity, Max could see displaced remnants of rocks and soil from placer mining.

He parked in his assigned spot, then let Opal out on a long lead. "Dog first, then we'll go in," he told Katerina.

She had shifted sideways in the seat and drawn her few belongings into her lap. "No hurry. It's kind of embarrassing to check in using a pillow-case for luggage. I suppose I should be thankful it's not a plastic grocery sack."

"They know you're with me and I'm working here. Nobody will think anything of it." He quirked a smile. "I take it your former lifestyle didn't include a lot of making do with what was at hand."

"Don't hold that against me, okay? I'm learning the hard way."

"I can see that. Too bad you don't have extended family you can call on for help."

She huffed and jumped down. "I don't even have many friends these days. The only ones who still speak to me are the folks from my church, and even they seem a little standoffish. I suppose they're as confused as you are."

"You think I'm confused?" He locked the truck and led the way to the front porch past wild poppies, roses and tufts of gray-leafed lavender.

"I think you're deluded," Katerina replied. "You've been around so many lowlife thugs you don't recognize an honest person when you meet one."

"Meaning you?"

"Yes."

They passed through the door into a foyer. Fans kept the warm, dry air moving and made the ambient temperature tolerable. Max checked the box for his room and found a key for an additional room, as Dylan had promised.

He handed it to Katerina. "Here you go. Opal and I are right next door in room 203 so you'll be perfectly safe." A slight smile lifted one corner of his mouth despite his desire to squelch it. "Want help with your luggage?"

"Very funny." Tossing the sack over her shoulder she added, "I feel like a hobo ready to hop a freight."

"No railroad tracks up here in the hills. Sorry," Max quipped. "I'll see you to your room."

"I can manage."

His smile faded. "I know you can. I just want to be certain you get there. The last time I turned my back on you somebody tried to push you off a cliff."

"Surely there's no danger here."

"Opal and I do a sweep of the whole house twice a day," Max told her. "We'll check your room again now."

"You're scaring me."

"Good. I saw you keep a cool head in an emergency today but that's no reason to become complacent. Even smart, capable people can be fooled."

"*Now* you're getting the right idea about me," Katerina said with a grin. "About time."

Max saw no advantage to telling her he'd been citing failures in his own past rather than referring to hers. The scar on his cheek reminded him every morning when he shaved. That wasn't necessarily a bad thing. It paid to stay alert and doubt everything. Everybody. Too bad that hadn't been enough to keep agent Morrow safe.

Forensics proved Jake had been wounded in the shootout during the raid on the Duprees when

Reginald Dupree was captured. Since Reginald's uncle Angus had abducted Jake and escaped the dragnet by helicopter, it was surprising there had been no ransom demands. Of course, Jake was resourceful and may have escaped. Max's worry was that he hadn't returned to headquarters or contacted Quantico because he was hurt or otherwise physically unable.

And then there was Esme Dupree. She'd been in witness protection until she'd panicked and run from her handlers, too. Without her testimony it was possible they'd have trouble getting a murder conviction for her brother, Reginald, although he and his underlings were sure to spend time in prison on drug charges. If Max had thought it would be feasible to sway the second sister, Violetta, he'd have felt a lot more positive about satisfactorily wrapping up the entire case. One phone call to her had proved that she intended to be anything but cooperative. The minute he'd asked her about Esme she'd hung up on him. No doubt she feared her family. Too bad she wasn't as brave as her missing sister.

Which focused his thoughts on the crime family and the random bombings. And therefore on Katerina. She was standing in front of the door to her room, key in hand, waiting for him. She looked...

Max set his jaw. She looked as innocent as a lamb with her big, guileless blue eyes and that wavy golden hair. Part of him wanted to believe her. Another part warned that even lambs could hide the spirit of a ravenous wolf.

The room Katerina had been given was charming. It was dwarfed by her boudoir at the ranch but far surpassed it in lovely decor and a sense of home. Moreover, someone had carefully folded and arranged clean clothes for her atop the antique chest of drawers. That, alone, helped boost her spirits. The view from the lace-curtained window did, too. Raising the sash she was able to look out at rolling hills beyond the massive, gnarled oak that framed the scene. Its shade brought relief from the late afternoon sun while a mild breeze ruffled its leaves and soothed her spirit.

A soft knock at her door was startling. "Who is it?"

"Room service."

The deep male voice sounded terribly familiar. When she opened the door a crack to peek out, her suspicions were confirmed. The very special agent stood in the hallway balancing a tray of food.

"I didn't order anything."

"You need to eat. And rest. Under the circumstances I thought it was sensible for you to dine in your room so you could kick back and unwind."

"And so you could keep an eye on me?" Katerina stepped back, holding the door for him.

"That, too." He placed the tray on a small table by the window. "You have to keep up your strength. I've contacted the diner where you work and explained that you'll need a few days off. First thing tomorrow we'll head out to the ranch, get your stuff and look over the scene. My people didn't turn up anything but you may spot changes because the place is so familiar to you."

"Okay." When he hesitated instead of leaving, she wondered if he'd intended to eat with her. "There's enough for two, if you want to join me," she offered with a sweep of her arm.

"No, no. I won't be staying. Lock your door when I leave and keep it that way unless you notify me." He reached into his pocket and produced a small cell phone. "This is for you. My number is already programmed into it. Don't use it for anything else."

"I had a smartphone in my truck. Was that ruined, too?"

"Yes. According to the evidence techs."

She had other ideas. "You guys kept it to check my activity, didn't you? Well, have at it. I have nothing to hide and the sooner you figure that out, the better."

Max was backing toward the open door. "Good

night, then. Eat. Please? I really do want you to stay healthy."

"Because a feeble suspect is harder to explain?" Katerina laughed wryly. "Okay, okay. I'll take good care of myself. You won't have to make excuses for mistreating me." A smile remained as she studied the stalwart agent.

He frowned. "What's so funny?"

"Nothing. I was just realizing that I'm starting to like you. Given my terrible record for choosing friends, particularly of the male persuasion, I figure you're probably planning to arrest me soon and throw me in the slammer with good old Vern."

"The *slammer*?" Max chuckled. "You watch too many B movies."

"Old black-and-white ones are the best," Katerina said. "I love those."

"If you want comedy, maybe. Police work is nothing like that anymore."

"Imagine how it would have been if those characters had had cell phones and modern communications the way we do these days."

Max nodded toward the phone he had just given her. He was no longer smiling. "Keep that with you at all times. Understand?"

"Yes." She made a fist around it. "I don't know how to thank you—for this room and everything."

"You can start by naming your boyfriend's associates," he said flatly.

If Katerina had not been taken aback by the abrupt change in his demeanor she would have slammed the door instead of letting him close it quietly behind him.

She had never met anyone, human or animal, as hardheaded and stubborn as that impossible man. The only plus side she could see was that he was undoubtedly thinking the same kinds of thoughts about her. Well, good. It was about time somebody gave her credit for courage and backbone, even if it happened for the wrong reasons.

Circumstances had forced her into independence and the more she experienced, the better she felt about herself. That, alone, was a prime example of good resulting from disaster, just as the Bible promised. If someone had told her a month ago that she would be homeless, practically destitute and in mortal danger she would have laughed at them.

Now, however, she not only was not amused, she found herself calling upon an inner strength, a latent faith and trust in God, that she hadn't realized lay within.

SIX

Balmy night breezes lifted the lacy curtains over the window in Katerina's room. Because of the hilly terrain, semidarkness had arrived before true sunset. She was more than ready to rest. Matter of fact, she'd started to get really sleepy while eating at the small table in front of the window.

Wrapped in the cocoon of the summer night, she went to the canopied bed, stretched out on the cool sheets and let the humming of cicadas lull her to sleep. As long as the buzzing noise rose and fell in cadence, Katerina was at peace. When it abruptly stopped, however…

Her eyelids fluttered. She stirred, shifted position and stretched. "Umm. Thirsty."

There was half a carafe of iced tea left on the table from her evening meal, wasn't there? She yawned, then sat up and swung her legs over the side of the bed, taking a moment to get her bearings and straighten the T-shirt and shorts she'd chosen in lieu of proper nightclothes.

Quiet was welcome, of course, but something about the total silence bothered her. No insects were buzzing and other than the occasional hoot of an owl, night birds were silent, too.

Katerina paused to listen. To think. The narrow road that wound past the B and B was mostly dark but headlights occasionally shined through her window as cars followed the twisted street.

Fine hairs at the nape of her neck prickled a warning. Logic argued against fear yet instinct insisted she take care despite the fact that her door was locked and an FBI agent was lodged in the room next door.

She could hear herself breathing, feel the thump of her pulse as if that, too, were audible. Maybe it was. Her heart was certainly beating hard and fast enough.

A single, deep bark startled her. She tensed even more. The sound had not come from outside; she'd heard it through the wall from Max's room. Opal? Why would she bark when everything else was so seemingly peaceful?

Slowly, cautiously, Katerina began to reach toward the pillow at the head of her bed. The special cell phone was tucked under it. Whether she used the phone or not, it would be comforting to have it in hand.

The rumble of a motor outside grew closer. Another car was passing. Katerina instinctively glanced in the direction of the open window—and saw a shadow.

It froze for a split second, then began to move, to grow larger. It was inside and coming toward her!

She crab-walked backward across the bed. "No! Get away from me."

"Too bad you woke up. I was just going to leave you a note but since you're awake, we can have a little talk."

"No."

A hand snaked out of the dimness and grabbed her ankle. *Caught*!

Twisting and kicking, she clawed to reach the cell phone. The more she fought, the farther away from it the prowler pulled her.

"Let go of me."

Realizing how inane it was to argue with someone who had invaded her room and was threatening her, she resorted to the kind of ear-piercing, inarticulate scream she'd heard only in scary movies—and from herself during the incident in her hospital room.

It caused her attacker to loosen his hold. She continued to screech until he turned and scrambled for the open window.

Intent on escape herself, Katerina ran for help, twisted the bolt, threw the open the door and crashed into her FBI protector.

* * *

Max staggered back, kept his balance and grabbed her. "What happened?"

Katerina merely pointed into her room.

Rushing in with Opal at his side, Max checked the small suite in seconds. When he looked back, Katerina was standing in the doorway with her arms folded, hugging herself. "The window," was all she said.

Max leaned out, satisfied himself that the threat had fled, then returned to her. By that time, several other guests of the establishment as well as the concerned owners had gathered in the hallway.

He shooed them away. "It's all right. Everything is under control. It was just a bad dream."

"Bad dream my eye." Katerina was almost shouting. "There was somebody in my room. I saw him. He threatened me and grabbed me."

Slipping an arm around her shoulders, Max sought to comfort and quiet her. "Take it easy, Ms. Garwood. Opal and I will look after you." Again, he addressed the small group. "You can all go back to sleep. My apologies for the disturbance."

"Well I'm not going to stay in there," Katerina said in a quavering voice as the others left. "Not when somebody has already found me."

Max turned her to face him and spoke quietly. "I understand. You can take my room and I'll sleep in yours. But right now I need more details. Tell me what you saw."

"There was a shadow. It came at me in the dark." She shivered. "I tried to reach the phone to call for help but he grabbed my ankle and started to pull me off the bed."

"Did he say anything?"

"I don't… Yes! He said he'd been about to leave me a note."

"All right. When I checked your room I was looking for a person, not evidence. Stay where you are while I look again."

"Not on your life. Where you and that dog go, I go. I heard her bark when I was about to be attacked. She must have heard something."

"That was what woke me." Unwilling to argue when he could see Katerina trembling with fear, Max led the way into her room, leaving the door ajar. Supper dishes remained on the table by the window. A carafe of tea had been knocked over and liquid was puddled on the floor. Amid the chaos was a folded piece of white paper.

Max pointed. "Is that yours?"

"No, I…" She started to reach for it. He stayed her hand. "Leave it. There may be fingerprints."

Katerina studied her ankle. "I doubt it. I think I felt gloves, not bare skin."

"Whatever." He lifted the folded paper with two fingers at a corner and laid it on a bare spot atop the dresser, then used a pencil to carefully unfold it. If it had been the kind of threat an innocent person usually received he might have kept Katerina from reading it. Instead, he stepped back and watched her reactions as she scanned the note.

"Turn over the stash and we'll leave you alone?" she read aloud. "What's that supposed to mean? I don't know anything about any stash. Do they mean drugs?"

"Your guess is better than mine," Max countered evenly. "What do you think?"

She threw up her hands and began to pace. "How should I know? I don't have a clue."

"I wish I could believe you."

"Yeah," Katerina said, scowling at the piece of paper, "I wish you could, too."

Max escorted Katerina back to his room and left her there with Opal. She knew he and the local police would be going over her original room with magnifying glasses, looking for clues, and was relieved to have a refuge away from their investigation.

It was also comforting to have the trained K-9 for company, although at the moment Opal was acting more like a house pet than a police officer. "Must be because you're out of uniform, huh?"

Katerina said tenderly. "Your partner did say you were different when you knew you were working."

The boxer's stubby tail wagged, making the rear half of her body move in sync. "Australian shepherds are just like you," she cooed. "When they wag they wag all over. You'd like the dogs at the ranch. They're lots of fun."

Perching on the only chair in the room, Katerina let Opal rest her heavy head on her knee. "You're a sweet girl, aren't you? Yes, you are. Does your partner ever scratch behind your ears like this?" She demonstrated. "Do you like that?"

If the boxer could have replied, Katerina knew she'd have agreed, because the expression of pleasure in her dark brown eyes was evident.

Touching the animal helped calm Katerina, too. Medical science had long claimed that stroking a dog or cat had a beneficial effect on the human body. She believed it.

So did having a pet as a companion. If she hadn't had her horses to train and the ranch dogs underfoot when her mother had passed away, she didn't know how she'd have coped.

Yes, she relied on her faith to carry her through trying times, but as far as Katerina was concerned, God used his earthly creatures to augment His ministrations. And why not? They were a part of His creation, just as she was.

That thought brought her musings back to

Special Agent West. He was special, all right. The look on his face when she'd run into the hallway had proved his true concern despite words to the contrary. He might put forth the image of a hard-boiled cop but there was a kind man inside. She knew that without question. The element she doubted was whether she'd ever be able to convince him to let down his guard and see her as she truly was—innocent and worthy of befriending.

Or more? she asked herself, blushing. Yes, Max was older than Vern had been but given her disastrous experiences in regard to that relationship, maturity was certainly a plus. Not to mention how good-looking he was.

Could she get past Max's original attacks on her? Others had said far worse and had hurt her deeply. She might not respect her dad the way she once had, but that didn't mean she'd stopped loving him. The same went for her friends. Anybody could make a mistake. She certainly had. Forgiveness was the key.

Sleep eluded Katerina until almost dawn. She wasn't certain Opal was allowed on the bed but decided to permit the welcome company.

Sighing, she started to smile and made eye contact with the dog as it lay on its back, all four legs in the air. "You snore. Did you know that?" The smile grew as the boxer's tongue fell out of the side of her mouth and she started to pant. "Yes, you do so don't try to deny it."

A light rap on wood brought Opal to instant alertness. Tail end wagging, she leaped down, ran to the door and barked once.

"Come in."

"Why didn't you check to see who it was?" Max demanded. "And why wasn't your door locked like I told you?"

"Good morning to you, too, Special Agent Grumpy. I wanted help to be able to get to me if I was threatened again. And Opal was right here to defend me."

"That's actually sort of logical." He raked his fingers through short, damp hair. "Sorry. Long night."

"Same here," Katerina said. "Your dog snores."

"Like a freight train," he agreed, starting to smile. "You up for breakfast? I can take Opal for her walk while you go back to your room and get dressed."

"Fine." She eyed her current attire. "These aren't pj's but they aren't exactly traveling clothes, either. Are we still going back to the ranch today?"

"That was my plan."

Judging by the way he was loitering she assumed he had more to say. "What is it? You look like a man with a secret."

"I got a match on the prints we took off that warning note from last night."

"Wonderful! Who was it?"

"Vern Kowalski," Max said flatly.

Gaping at him, Katerina stammered, "H-how is that possible?"

"We're not sure. The only way that can be is if Vern handled the paper sometime before he was arrested and left his prints then."

"So whoever wrote the note has to be someone he knew."

"That's what it looks like."

"Then ask him. Your people need to make him talk." She pressed her lips together and gave Max a frigid look. "Just leave me out of it, okay? I never want to lay eyes on the skunk again—apologies to the real animal."

"Normally, that would be a good idea," Max said quietly.

She noted how seriously he seemed to be studying her as he added, "Unfortunately, we can't. Vern Kowalski was murdered in the exercise yard early this morning. Nobody is going to be getting any more information out of him."

Katerina sank back against the edge of the mattress and grabbed the bedpost for support. "No."

"I'm sorry for your loss," Max said gruffly.

Although she was filled with mixed emotions, one rose to prominence. "I'm sorry for *every-*

body's loss," she clarified. "Because now there is no way you can find out what's been going on."

She straightened, pulled herself together and met his gaze boldly even though her heart was pounding. "Worse, there's no chance I'll be exonerated until you catch all the criminals who are involved." An eyebrow arched as she added, "And one of them is *not* me."

"I'm beginning to believe you," Max replied slowly.

Katerina let herself smile in relief. "Well, it's about time."

SEVEN

Max wasted no time loading Opal into the SUV with Katerina and heading for the Garwood Ranch. Now that Kowalski was out of the picture it was possible that Bertrand Garwood would reconsider his harsh stand. On the other hand, there was an equal chance the man would gloat and make things worse for Katerina. She may have washed her hands of her former fiancé but there had to be some lingering sorrow over his demise. After all, she'd been within days of marrying him. That helped explain her reluctance to accept his position in law enforcement, he supposed. Even a totally innocent person would feel uneasy if they found themselves under the microscope of the US government.

In a way, Katerina's situation reminded him of Dylan's fiancee, Zara Fielding, who had become involved in some kind of mystery while training at Quantico. If an honest person like her could wind up embroiled in trouble without being a participant, so could Katrina.

Clouds kept the sun at bay and temperatures temporarily lower than usual. Rain would be welcome on the tinder-dry grass and brush as long as lightning strikes didn't kindle fires. There was always a chance of that, particularly when thunder and lightning preceded any moisture, according to the fire chief.

"Odd weather, isn't it?" he asked.

"Not good. They postponed our South Fork Founder's Day parade at the end of May because bad storms were forecast. As dry as everything is, the last thing we need is a spark to set it all on fire." Max was surprised to see her smile until she added, "Dad was livid. He was supposed to ride in a convertible as mayor and show how important he is."

"Have they rescheduled? Rain or no rain, it could be dangerous for him to put himself out there like that."

"He wouldn't care. Not when he has a chance to flaunt his political position and wave to all the civilians."

Having met the man, Max understood perfectly. "If we haven't managed to arrest whoever has been harassing you before then, I'll try to talk some sense into him."

"Seriously? You'd do that?"

"Sure. Why not?" He paused to regroup his thoughts. "That is if I'm still in California. Opal is technically a bomb detecting K-9. If the threat disappears from here, I'll either go back to Billings or move on to the next assignment."

Katerina turned to study him. "I'm confused. Are you after a gang of drug dealers or chasing bombings?"

"Well…"

"You may as well level with me, Agent West. The internet is full of speculation and so are local newspapers. Their conclusions point to a connection and blame the Dupree crime family for everything."

"That is highly possible."

"Which is where my former—um, where Vern comes in?"

He glanced her way. "He's one common element. He worked for Dupree."

"And Dad's stable just blew up."

"I already told you, Ms. Garwood, I doubt that anybody who was looking for hidden loot, the way the warning note says, would take the chance of setting a bomb anywhere the drugs might be cached. That would be idiotic."

"Are you giving criminals too much credit for using their brains?"

Max shrugged. "Maybe. It's often easier to track a smart crook who's predictable than to find one who acts on a whim. Take these bombings for instance. If you look at them on a map, patterns show up. People don't mean to reveal their inner thoughts but they do so just the same. It's almost impossible for a rational thinker to act in a totally random manner." He wheeled beneath the fancy iron arch and entered Garwood Ranch. "Here we are."

"Yeah." She breathed a noisy sigh. "Well, let's get this over with. I don't want to stay one second longer than I absolutely have to."

"You can't be afraid of your father, not after the way you've handled yourself since we met. You were amazing on the broken stairs. And last night—you didn't get hysterical or even cry."

"I'm less sad about my dad's choices than I am disappointed," Katerina said softly. "I thought he loved me. I thought Vern did, too. Guess I'm not very perceptive."

"There's nothing wrong with putting your trust in someone," Max murmured as he pulled through the yard and parked next to the remnants of the destroyed stable building. "The secret is in choosing who is deserving and who isn't."

"How do *you* do it?" Katerina glanced at the threatening clouds as she got out and joined him.

Max chuckled and shook his head, "Poorly."

"Why? Because you kept doubting me?"

"Yes, and no." He leashed Opal and put her to

work while they made small talk. "I tend to doubt everybody. Everything. It's a valuable trait for my job, but it doesn't make for a lot of friends."

"You're not married, are you?"

"No. Why?" The scowl he sent her way was meant to end their conversation. It seemed to have the opposite effect.

"I'm sorry. It must be lonely, traveling all over the country with nobody waiting for you at home. I never realized how much I relied on friends and family until I had to face the loss of most of them. The loneliness is astounding. I hadn't dreamed it would hurt so much."

"I have my job and Opal. That's enough."

Following the K-9 as she skirted the pile of rubble, nose to the ground, Max was glad he wasn't facing Katerina when she said, "No. It isn't."

Katerina sensed friction in the air between her and Max so she kept her distance. It was none of her business what kind of private life Agent West chose to live, she just hated to see anyone unhappy. Oh, he was capable and intelligent and wonderful hero material, but inside he seemed wanting, as if his heart were silently calling for help. For companionship.

"I am certifiable," she muttered to herself. "Why should I care about a guy who was ready to throw me in jail before he even met me?"

Because you both are lonely and need each other, her subconscious answered. Of course there was no way she and Max could ever become a couple. Innocent or not, her name was stained by her prior associations just as her father had claimed. Still, the ruggedly handsome agent was growing more appealing daily and the possibility of romance kept popping into her head.

Letting her thoughts ramble, she wandered behind the part of the stable building left standing and came to an abrupt halt. Katerina stared. Her heart sank and angry, bitter tears filled her eyes.

Two cardboard boxes sat atop a pile of soot, dirt and barn sweepings and in those boxes was the proof of her entire career as a successful trainer and rider. Her trophies were smashed as if someone had taken a hammer to them. And the ribbons and beautiful rosettes? They were mired in filth. How *dare* he!

Katerina spun on her heel and headed for the house. Outrage fueled her courage and anger drove her forward. Behind her she heard Max calling. She ignored him. Bertrand Garwood was going to answer for his vindictive disregard of her feelings. Today.

Max was startled to see Katerina marching across the open space between the house and stables. Her actions went against everything she had told him. If she wanted to avoid confronting her father she was definitely headed in the wrong direction.

Drawing Opal close to his side Max began to jog. "Katerina! Wait."

She didn't slow her pace. If anything, she sped up. Several ranch hands paused to watch her from a distance but nobody else tried to interfere.

Max broke into a run. "Stop!"

He overtook her just as she reached the elaborate front entrance and raised a fist to bang on the door. Max's firm grip on her wrist stopped her. Fury in her glance made him let go. "Take a breath and tell me what's wrong."

"My—my awards," she stammered, her lower lip quivering. "He trashed them all."

"I don't understand."

"I used to compete and show our horses. I was good. I had the trophies and ribbons to prove it." She raised one arm to point toward the stables. "I'd gathered them all up to take with me when I came for the rest of my things. They're back behind the barns in a pile of…"

He gritted his teeth and eyed the roiling clouds. "Wind's coming up. If we intend to salvage anything before it rains we'd better get a move on."

"It's too late. They're all ruined."

"Maybe we can save something." He had to bite back his fury at anyone would destroy the dreams and accomplishments of another the way Garwood had. "Did you dig through and actually make sure, or are you assuming?"

"I couldn't bring myself to look closely," Katerina admitted. "I suppose there could be a few ribbons I can wash and keep as mementos."

He slipped an arm around her shoulders and urged her to turn with him. "Then let's go. I'll help you sort it all out."

"What about looking for clues to the explosion?"

"I'm done. It didn't take Opal long to tell me the area is clean. Whatever residue there may have been was widely scattered when they put out the fire. She showed mild interest in a couple of stalls but that's all."

"It seems pretty impossible for her to find clues at all, let alone after so many people and animals have tramped through your crime scenes."

Max was glad Katerina was starting to calm down and think more rationally. "That's where her sense of smell comes in handy. I've seen her locate tiny pieces of detonators, for instance, amid whole piles of refuse. She's really amazing."

Thunder rumbled in the distance. Men who had been working inside metal-fenced outdoor pens began to gather their tools. The air was crackling as dangerous lightning sought a connection to the ground. Formerly curious farm dogs scattered and took cover.

Katerina broke into a trot with Max and Opal at her side and led the way. "Back here."

He kept pace until they reached the box of ruined trophies. Opal stopped him with a pull to the left that nearly jerked him off his feet. She'd found a separate box that neither human had noticed.

"Katerina. Wait. Look," Max called. "What's this?"

"My clothes!" She started to reach for the large cardboard carton.

Max's outstretched arm stopped her. "Hold on. Opal thinks there may be something wrong."

"With my stuff?"

He had to tell her, "Yes."

"Terrific. Now what?"

"You take the ribbons into the barn to keep them out of the rain and sort them while I examine this."

"You're trying to get rid of me, aren't you?" Her pulse quickened. "How risky is it?"

"If I thought Opal had actually identified an explosive device I'd be the first one to call for a bomb squad. Unfortunately, there isn't anything like that in South Fork or even Oakhurst so we'd have a long wait."

Her hand gripped his arm, her nails digging in. "It's better than getting blown up."

Max looked to his K-9 partner. She was curious about the second carton but not behaving as if she smelled volatile substances.

"Don't worry about me," Max said with a reassuring smile. "Whatever she senses in there isn't going to go boom."

"You know that how?"

"I trust Opal. If she were sitting next to it and looking at me for praise, we'd both make a run for it."

"No offense, but I think I'll take your first suggestion and go to the barn. I'd like to say hello to my favorite horse, anyway."

"Fine with me." He handed her the end of the leash. "Take Opal with you."

"Why? I thought you said it was safe out here."

"From the box, not from the storm," Max explained. "I'll join you two in a few minutes."

"You'd better," Katerina warned, "or I'll call Sheriff Tate."

"Just hold your horses."

"Is that a pun?"

His grin widened. "It wasn't intended to be but if you think it's funny, fine. Now go, before we both get soaked."

"Okay, okay. I'm going."

Drops the size of dimes began to dot the dry ground and the partially folded flaps of the box of clothing. Max grabbed a pitchfork and used its tines to push the top farther open. Katerina was right. All there seemed to be was a jumble of shirts and jeans. A hairbrush and toothbrush lay on top, apparently tossed in last.

He stood back and studied the visible contents. Perhaps Opal had smelled Katerina on the items. Then again, maybe he was missing something. But what?

The answer turned out to be close enough to touch. Max, however, did not. Using a plastic evidence bag between his fingers and the folded piece of paper that was tucked beneath Katerina's hairbrush, he lifted it out. The lab would tell him for sure if this was a note like the one he'd found in her room at the hotel. The paper looked the same. So did the manner in which it was creased. If he chose to open it he'd be able to guess whether or not the handwriting matched. Proper tests would tell him if the paper was tainted with explosives. Or with drugs. Hefting the box, note and all, he headed for the barn where Katerina and Opal waited. His first instinct was to keep the news of another note to himself but he quickly changed his mind. Nothing the young woman had done or said since he'd met her had indicated guilt, not even by association. Assuming she truly was in danger she deserved to see what was written. This note had been left for her after all, and she had a right to read it.

And there was another benefit. He was going to be able to judge more about her character as he observed her initial reactions.

Katerina was renewing her friendship with Moonlight when Opal began to wiggle, whine and tug on her leash. Max was back. And he had brought the box of clothing.

"Oh, good. I was afraid you were going to say that was evidence and keep it."

"Some of it, I am," he countered grimly.

"Give me a break. What can my clothes have to do with bombs?"

"I don't know yet." Depositing the carton atop stacked hay bales, he said, "The top shirt and the hairbrushes will stay with me. You can have the stuff underneath, providing there aren't more notes tucked in down there."

Her breath caught. "Notes? You found more notes?"

"One. And it's possible that whoever left it had to move your brushes to put it there, so they'll have to be checked for prints before I can let you have them."

"What does this one say?"

"I don't know yet." He displayed the plastic baggie. "I didn't unfold it."

She lunged. "Well, I will," but he was too quick and held it out of reach.

"I'm going to lay a larger sheet of clean plastic on this hay bale, then open the note with tweezers. Before I do, I'll need your promise to not touch it."

"I promise." What choice did she have? He was the federal agent with all the authority. She was a mere civilian. Besides, she didn't want to contaminate possible evidence. Each opportunity took them one step closer to solving the mystery of her stalker.

"Okay. Shut those sliding doors at the end of the aisle so the wind doesn't blow through. It's getting nasty out there."

"Right." Katerina ran to follow his instructions. He was right about the increasing wind. Rain was now being blown against one end of the long, rectangular building and making a staccato patter.

She returned to him. "We should have parked your SUV inside so we wouldn't get wet."

"It wasn't raining when we got here."

"Are you always so logical?"

"I try to be." Although he was concentrating on unfolding the note, he took time to add, "You should try it sometime. It might simplify your life."

She huffed. "Nothing will ever fix my life. You know it and I know it. Vern's lies have ruined my past, my present and probably my future, and there's nothing I can do about it."

Expecting him to argue, Katerina was disappointed when he didn't. What he did do was smooth the note with another baggie and hold down the closest corner so they could both see the text.

I want the goods, it said. *Turn them over or you'll end up like your boyfriend.*

Katerina took a backward step. "They must think I hid drugs for Vern."

"I'm going to phone the jail and see if anybody was with Kowalski to hear his last words."

"Besides his killer, you mean? Do you think that's why he was murdered? Could he have been tortured for information?"

"If the Duprees think he was double-crossing them, then yes, it's a possibility. He may have tried to skim or steal and died before he revealed where he'd stashed the loot."

Katerina felt woozy. She leaned against the half door of Moonlight's stall and stroked the horse's velvety nose, drawing comfort from the contact while she mulled over her dilemma.

"This drug cartel thinks I know."

"That's how it looks," he said on a rough exhale. "Are you sure he never said anything about keeping some deep dark secret?"

"Not a peep. No clues, no hints, nothing. I thought he sold insurance, remember?"

This time, when Max nodded and looked steadily at her, Katerina could tell he was on her side. That was huge. She had a true ally. A defender. They might not yet be friends, nor were they romantically involved despite her covert appreciation of Max's many fine attributes. But that didn't matter.

God had answered her fervent prayers. She had been sent a special agent who had finally seen the truth and believed in her innocence. She no longer had to stand alone.

EIGHT

As far as Max was concerned he'd remain in California until all threats to Katerina were neutralized. Higher-ups in the FBI, however, disagreed. He was ordered back to Billings when a credible lead to the whereabouts of Jake Morrow was texted to headquarters.

"Are you sure this isn't another wild-goose chase?" he asked when Dylan O'Leary contacted him. "I want to find Jake as much as the next guy but it's really iffy to leave here now."

"Afraid it's out of your hands, Boss. We've had several reliable sightings of Agent Morrow in the past few days besides the latest tip." The tech guru sounded a lot more somber than usual.

"Okay. I trust your judgment. Tell me again what the message said."

Dylan read it verbatim.

"Daddy's home but not for long. Catch him if you can."

"What makes you think that pertains to Jake?" Max demanded. "It could mean anybody."

"True. But think about it. The only daddy directly involved in the Dupree case is Jake and he was supposedly spotted by several witnesses. It all fits."

"People claim to have seen him all over the country. Prove to me that text has anything to do with the Duprees and I might take it more seriously. Have you been able to trace the source of the message?"

"Not well. It came from a burner phone but the signal did bounce off a tower near the Dupree estate. They may have a snitch in their midst."

"That would be too good to be true." Max made his decision. "All right. I'll fly back and leave my vehicle here. That way I'll have to come back for it."

"Unless they decide to have it transported. When shall we expect you?"

"Book me a direct flight. My closest airport is probably San Jose."

"Affirmative." O'Leary lowered his voice to a personal level. "Listen, buddy, I understand how you feel about leaving Cali right now. It almost killed me when Zara went off to Quantico. And then when her friend went missing, it was worse."

Max's forehead knit. "I don't know what you mean."

"Sure you do. I've been handling all your special requests, remember?" A chuckle. "You've got a thing for that Garwood woman and you know it."

"Don't be ridiculous."

"Suit yourself. You can deny emotional involvement all you want but I've never known you to hesitate one second to follow orders before. If she's not the reason, what is?"

"Opal is being utilized here almost daily. As long as bombs are being set, this is where she belongs."

"Yeah, well, we haven't been napping, either. Harper has canvassed neighbors in the coverage area of the cell tower and she's come up with a few strong leads. We haven't called for a full-out police action because we don't want to tip anyone off."

"I suppose it's possible that whoever placed the call is near where Jake's being held captive."

"True. Plus, Harper has a name and possible location for Morrow's baby mama. She's requested Opal as backup in case there's a problem."

"Why didn't you say so in the first place?" Max was pacing, throwing clothing into a pile on the bed while Opal watched. "I'll be packed in a few minutes and on my way. Allow me three or four hours to drive to the airport."

"Copy. What're you going to do about the Garwood woman?"

Hesitating, Max looked toward Katerina's room as if he could see through the solid wall. "I'm not sure. She's going to want to go back to work soon so I wouldn't be able to watch her 24/7 anyway. I'll need to arrange transportation for her while I'm gone. Something inconspicuous with a powerful engine. See what you can do, will you?"

Dylan chuckled. "You give me a lot of credit. Anything else? Bodyguards, maybe?"

"No, but that is a good idea. I'll speak to the local sheriff and see if he can spare a unit to escort her to and from work. It's not far."

"You are so transparent," the techie said, laughing more. "How many other crime victims have you decided to protect no matter what? One? Two? None?"

"I would have if I'd thought it was necessary," Max argued. "While I'm in Billings I want you to be tracking down leads to who is responsible for offing Kowalski in jail. Find out if the guy lived long enough to have spoken to anybody and see if you can tie that person to the Duprees."

"You think it was more than random prison violence?"

"Absolutely. I've sent the warning notes Ms. Garwood received to Quantico. Find out what they discovered and be sure the report reaches me.

Even if there are no readable fingerprints on the paper there may be trace evidence that will help."

"Okay. I'll get back to you as soon as I book your flight."

"Thanks." Max realized he was concerned beyond normal, yet refused to consider that Dylan might be right about his personal involvement. Katerina was not only from a different world, that of wealth and privilege, she was too young for him. Still, he worried about her despite mental arguments to the contrary. It may be the human thing to do but it certainly was not a professional response. Not only was she on his mind almost constantly, he kept having to squelch the urge to pick up the phone and call her for no reason.

Well, *now* he had one. He pushed the button to speed-dial the phone he'd given her and prayed she'd understand why he had to virtually abandon her.

The unfamiliar ring startled Katerina. "Hello?"

"How are you this morning?" Max asked cautiously.

The tone of his voice was off somehow. "I'm okay. What's wrong?"

"Nothing, really. Why?"

"Because you don't sound normal. Have you figured out who is stalking me and what they want?"

"I have our best people working on that," he reassured her.

"Good. I want to go back to living my life. First I have to see if they can fix my truck, then I need to either find a new apartment or ask the landlord to repair the damage to my old one."

"I'd like you to stay where you are for the present. I'm making arrangements for a rental car."

She was both astounded and adamant. "No way. I can't afford it. You know that."

"I know. But I have to fly to Montana for a few days and I'd like to know you're safe, with plenty of people around you."

"You're *leaving*?" Part of her heart felt lodged in her throat while the rest plunged into her stomach and lay there like a boulder.

"Orders," he said flatly.

"I—I thought you were the boss. Special agent in charge and all that."

"There are higher-ups who can override my decisions. You'll be fine while I'm gone. I'll speak to the sheriff and have a deputy escort you to and from work."

What could she say? What could she do? She had no real hold on him other than an intense desire to remain in his company. Of course he had to follow orders. That only made sense. What was far less plausible was the ache developing within her as she contemplated his absence.

Katerina pulled herself together. "Of course. I understand. Do you intend to return to South Fork?"

"Definitely. We have the bombing at the ranch to keep looking at, plus the personal threats you've received. This is one time when your connection to the Dupree cartel is working in your favor."

"I guess I could look at it that way. Might as well have something good come out of my mistakes."

"Everybody makes them," Max told her gently.

Cradling the phone against her cheek she pretended he was speaking directly to her and was standing close, letting her draw on his strength the way she had before.

"Is it all right if I use this phone to call you while you're gone?" Katerina held her breath, hoping he'd say yes.

"Of course. I'll be checking in with you on a regular basis, too…" he cleared his throat "…in case you can remember any names or receive further threats. I doubt you'll be bothered with a visible police presence. When I get back we'll dig deeper into the mystery of where Vern hid whatever the stalkers are after."

"Promise?" It galled Katerina that her voice sounded weak at that moment. She was strong and capable. There was no reason to feel so lost while contemplating Max's absence. Yet she did. It was as if someone had blasted away the foundation of her stability, of her courage, and left her trying to stand on loose sand that kept shifting beneath her.

His "I promise" seemed sincere as well as heartfelt. That helped. So did the idea of going back to work soon. Her current situation required gainful employment and her psyche insisted that she make her own way despite obstacles. That was the mindset that had helped her succeed at training hardheaded horses and it would sustain her now.

"When do you leave?" she asked thickly.

"In a few minutes."

"Meet me in the hall so I can say goodbye to Opal?"

"Sure."

There was not a whisper of doubt in Katerina's mind that she wanted to give her staunch protector a parting hug. Whether she would be able to muster the courage to do so or whether Max would accept the gesture was the real question.

She had often pictured herself close to him the way she had been when he'd helped her leave the hospital. Every second he was near she wanted to lean on his broad shoulder or step into his embrace. The desire was more a matter of needing support than anything else, including romance, she insisted. That would be nice, of course, but at this point she mostly craved something that had been sorely lacking in her recent experiences. True moral support.

She did not intend to wilt like a delicate flower on a hot day and throw herself at him. After all, she was much stronger than that. But she also didn't intend to let him leave without conveying a hint of her growing affection. If she scared him away, so be it. He'd probably leave anyway. Eventually. So what did she have to lose—except her self-respect, and there wasn't a whole lot of that left over after recent events.

Grabbing the door handle she twisted the latch and stepped into the hall.

Max was waiting with Opal by his side. The sight of him was so endearing, so incredibly special, Katerina almost ran to him. Supreme effort slowed her pace. She began to smile.

As if they had both read the same script and were acting their parts, he pivoted to face her and opened his arms slightly.

That was all the invitation Katerina needed. Stepping up, she slid her arms around his waist, laid her head on his shoulder and closed her eyes. Words were unnecessary. Actions said all there was to say.

The flight to Billings was uneventful. By keeping Opal in uniform Max was able to walk her into the passenger compartment at his side without question. They were about to land when he received word from Dylan that Agent Harper Prentiss had verified the name and current location of Jake Morrow's girlfriend and was waiting for him at the airport.

Since he hadn't checked any luggage he was able to deplane and join her without delay.

They shook hands as their dogs sniffed each other and renewed acquaintance. "I hear you think you know where Jake's family is," Max said.

"Yes. It looks good. I'd just rather have Opal check the premises before Star and I go in, especially since the Dupree family is involved." She passed him a white paper sack. "Here you go. Fresh from Petrov's bakery. I know how meager airplane food can be."

Max pulled out a sticky bun and dug in. "My favorite. Thanks." As soon as he'd swallowed, he asked, "Didn't you date Jake at one time?"

"Not exactly. He and I didn't mesh." She shook her head pensively. "He was persistent there for a while, but there was no way. Not for me."

"Interesting." Max tossed his bag into the back of her SUV and instructed Opal to get in one side as Harper put her German shepherd, Star, in the other. The handlers met in the front seat. "Bring me up to speed," Max said. "What all have you managed to put together?"

"Neighbors near the target house where the

woman and toddler live have been shown Jake's photo. Some think they saw him inside. A few insisted his hair was darker. They said the man in question was usually wearing dark glasses, even in the house, so they weren't sure about his eye color."

"What can you tell me about the mother and baby?"

"Her name is Penny Potter. She's a single mother raising a toddler son, Kevin, whose father's name is not listed on the birth certificate. That's why we had so much trouble tracking her down."

Max's jaw clenched. "Assuming you have the right woman. And that she knows something that may help us track down the men who kidnapped Jake. It's iffy that their sightings were accurate."

"I know. But I wanted Opal along to make sure we're not walking into a Dupree trap. Other units are going to stage down the street and stand by until we give the all clear. We'll also have overhead coverage from our chopper. If Jake is in there, like some of the neighbors have said, whoever has been holding him may be present, too. I don't understand why Jake would be with the woman, but we can't ignore possibilities, no matter how far-fetched."

"Fair enough." Max drew his fingers down his cheek. "I left in such a hurry I didn't have time to shave."

"Too busy with Ms. Katerina?"

His head snapped around. "O'Leary has a big mouth and a wild imagination."

Harper was smiling. "Hey, don't knock it. There's nothing wrong with romance, especially at our age. The clock is ticking."

"Not for Katerina. She's a lot younger than I am."

"So?" the female agent retorted. "You can't be after her fortune now that she's been disinherited. If you two hit it off, I say go for it."

"It's not that simple. She was mixed up with the wrong crowd. Even planned to marry one of them."

"One little mistake," Harper said with a wry smile.

Max stayed sober. "Her little mistake was murdered while in police custody where he should have been safe. Apparently, before he was arrested, he stole something the Duprees want back."

"Secret files, maybe? Cooked books?"

"Possibly. I had assumed it was drugs until somebody tossed Katerina's apartment and looked in places far too small to conceal a valuable stash. It could be a flash drive, I suppose. Whatever it is, it's not bulky like the packages of drugs or stacks of money she thinks they're after."

"Interesting. You know, if the father of this

baby really is Jake Morrow and we can get Penny Potter to talk, she may be able to shed light on a lot of unknowns in this case."

Nodding, Max said, "Remember, Jake is a victim, too. As for the Potter woman, she may have been fooled and taken advantage of just like Katerina was."

"You really do believe the Garwood woman is innocent, don't you?"

"Yes. Even if I wasn't a trained profiler I'd have come to that conclusion. There is no way anybody is a good enough actor to fool me. Katerina is one of the most honest, unassuming people I've ever met. I can just look into her eyes and tell."

The other agent laughed. "Oh, brother, do you have it bad. I can hardly wait to see a hardheaded guy like you take the fall."

"I'm not falling anywhere," Max argued. "This job is all the fulfillment I need or want. Now, shall we talk about something else?"

"Whatever. I thought sure you'd want to call California and see how things are going there." She glanced knowingly at his cell phone.

"I probably should," Max said, doing his best to ignore his companion when she started to snicker quietly.

Katerina answered on the second ring. "Max?"

"Hey. Just checking on you."

"I'm so glad."

There was a breathless quality to her voice that concerned him. "Are you okay?"

"Fine. I called my boss at the Miner's Grub diner and he said they were shorthanded this afternoon so I volunteered to fill in. And here I am. It's good to be back at work. I hated sitting in my room alone."

"Sorry I couldn't leave Opal to keep you company. We needed her here."

"More bombs?" Fear tinged her previously upbeat tone.

"Just taking proper precautions. Are you doing the same? Did they get you a good car? I know they didn't have much to choose from."

"It's fine," Katerina told him. "Big and ugly and powerful enough to earn me speeding tickets. I love everything about it except the color. It's dill pickle–green."

"Picky, picky, picky," he teased. "No problems? No suspicious people lurking?" *Please, say no.*

"Peaceful and quiet." She paused. "I wish the same for you. I've been praying for you since you left."

He was touched—and a little embarrassed for not relying on a faith he used to trust in every instance until it failed him. Twice. "Thanks. Keep your eyes open and don't hesitate to call 9-1-1 if anything looks out of place or makes you nervous. Okay?"

"Okay. Hear that bell? I have an order up. Can't let it get cold. Maybe we can talk again later?"

"You can count on it," he said softly. "Take care."

The moment he broke the connection Harper giggled. "Want to tell me again that you don't have feelings for that woman. I've known you for years and I have never heard that much tenderness in your voice. Never. You've got it bad, Max. Do yourself a favor and admit it before Katerina gets away from you."

NINE

Katerina had told Max the truth. It did feel good to be back at work where she could stay busy and keep from brooding.

The casual ambience of the tiny diner had surprised her when she'd first entered it in search of a job. The Miner's Grub was the kind of blue-collar joint her dad wouldn't have been caught dead in unless he was hunting for votes, which was one reason she had never discovered it herself.

"I was an awful snob," she murmured, smiling because she could now see her character fault and willingly change. These people were kind and friendly and down-to-earth in ways she had overlooked in the past. Now she saw them for the children of God that they were. All were equal and worthy in His sight.

The owner, manager and cook, Xavier Alvarez, pushed open the kitchen door and stuck his balding head through. "You doin' okay, Señorita Kate?"

"Fine. Thanks for letting me come back." She'd

been pouring coffee and the distraction of turning to talk to him caused her to slop some onto the long counter. "Oops. Sorry."

He laughed good-naturedly. "I'd say I missed my best waitress but I know how you feel about telling the whole truth, so I'll just say we're glad for your help."

"I will be the best someday," Katerina promised. "I learned how to make thousand-pound horses behave when I was just a kid. I'm sure I can master a coffeepot."

"*Muy bien.* Very good. How late can you stay? Doris has been sitting up with sick *niños* for two nights. I'm not sure I can talk her into taking second shift."

"I can handle a double," Katerina assured him, and she meant it. What did not occur to her until she'd spoken was having to drive back to the quaint hotel in the dark. The mere idea that she might have to do it without her planned escort gave her the shivers. Nevertheless, she would do what she had to do in order to keep her job and please her boss. Xavier had hired her when she'd known nothing about serving or prepping food. He'd simply seen someone in need and had provided a way for her to survive while retaining her dignity. She would not let him down.

Busing tables by the windows gave her a chance to keep an eye on the ugly green barge Max had rented for her. It was a typical grandma car. Just sitting behind the wheel made her feel fifty years older!

"Which probably helps disguise me," she told herself. But from whom? There was little doubt at this point that her prior association with Vern was at fault. If he had given her anything to keep for him she would have remembered. There was nothing—except her engagement ring, and it was so infinitesimal it had brought expressions of sympathy from some of her highbrow friends. That was another reason she had never questioned him about money or suspected he was raking it in via drug smuggling. Anybody who was that deep into the culture should have had plenty of spare cash to throw around.

A scruffy-looking, twentysomething customer seated at the counter motioned her over. Smiling, Katerina grabbed a fresh pot of coffee and approached him. "Refill?"

"Sure."

She'd topped off his cup and started to turn away when he stopped her with, "You're Vern's girl, aren't you?"

What was the point of denying it? "I used to be."

"That's what I thought. You don't remember me, do you? We met at a party down by the river last spring."

Vague recollections stirred but nothing definitive came to her. "Maybe."

"I'm Kyle," the wiry man said.

Katerina didn't like the way he was staring at her, but he wasn't the first customer who had gotten out of line since she'd started working at the diner. More experienced waitresses had told her to flirt and joke if she wanted good tips. In the case of this man, however, she saw no benefit, particularly since he'd already admitted to being a friend of Vern's. Any friend of Vern's was no friend of hers.

"How about a nice piece of pie with that coffee?" she asked for diversion. "We have apple, cherry, coconut cream…"

He reached for her.

Katerina avoided him with a step backward.

He crooked an index finger. "C'mere. I won't bite. I just want to give you a message from your boyfriend."

"I told you. I don't have a boyfriend."

"Funny. He thinks you do."

Was she the only one who knew that Vern had been killed? She supposed it was possible, but it seemed to her that his cronies should have gotten the news by now, particularly since criminals were privy to their own insider communications.

"Really?"

"Yeah," Kyle said with a half-smile. "And he

wants me to pick up the stuff he hid and turn it into cash for him."

"Oh?" Katerina decided to play along and see how far the man would go. He might even reveal some hint that would help her figure out what it was that she was supposed to know about. "What does that have to do with me?"

"He said he told you where he hid it."

"Somebody already trashed my apartment. Maybe they found what Vern wants."

Kyle's smile widened and he briefly averted his glance. "Uh, nope. That was me. Sorry."

"You're *sorry*?" She couldn't help showing ire. "I had to move because of the mess you made."

"Yeah, but you got better digs out of it. That nice big window gives you a great view, too."

To cover the trembling that had begun when he'd insinuated he was her stalker, she set the coffeepot on the prep counter behind her and folded her arms. "That was *you* in my hotel room, too?"

Kyle spread his hands in a gesture meant to convey innocence. Katerina wasn't buying it. "And you have the gall to come here and face me? You people are unbelievable. Haven't you ever heard of *asking*?"

"Hey, I asked. I left notes."

She'd reached the end of her patience. Placing both palms on the counter between them she leaned forward and spoke boldly, never taking her eyes off his disgustingly smug expression.

"Look, mister, I don't know what you want or where Vern may have left it, but he sure didn't tell me. If he had, I'd have turned it over to the police already. Got that?" It was clear he didn't believe her. "And you can stop pretending that Vern sent you, okay? You and I both know he's dead."

It did her good to see shock on the man's face. "He's what?"

"Dead. Murdered." Katerina had less trouble expressing herself about it now than she had at first. Acknowledging the loss of her imaginary happy future wasn't nearly as painful as it had been, undoubtedly because she had lost all faith in her fiancé long before his demise.

"When?"

"I heard about it yesterday. I'm surprised you don't already know. If you're tied to the same crime bosses he was, you should."

Kyle slid off the stool and began to back up, hands raised. "Hey, I'm just an innocent bystander trying to do a favor for a friend. If you're as smart as you think you are, you'll tell me where to find those rocks and save yourself a boatload of grief. Whoever arranged to off Vern will be after you, too. And your family."

"Rocks?"

Kyle lowered his voice. "You are either the

dumbest woman I've ever met or the best liar. The diamonds. Where did he hide them?"

Diamonds? No wonder her adversaries had been so persistent. Katerina's mind was whirling as the past weeks flashed by in memory. What was it that Max had said? Oh, yes. He'd been talking about the lack of reasoning behind the ranch explosion.

"So, if you wanted these diamonds, why did you blow up the stable at my dad's?" Katerina asked.

"What? Me? I didn't blow up nothin'."

Score another point for Special Agent West. She pressed her advantage. "Well, maybe you should find out who did because there's a fair chance that Vern hid what you're looking for at the ranch. He was out there all the time, visiting me and using my father's horse business as a transport for his drug smuggling. If he was going to hide anything he'd have had easy access."

Kyle was cursing under his breath. She could tell he was extremely nervous because his fists were clenched and he was twitching and shuffling like a racehorse in the starting gate.

When he finally made up his mind what to do and hurried toward the door, Katerina reached for his coffee mug, pinched the rim with two fingers and set it aside instead of placing it in the dirty dish bin to be taken to the kitchen and washed.

Max would be so proud of her, she thought, particularly if the stalker's fingerprints were on file. She didn't want to wait but the opportunity to present him with the evidence herself and see his smile was just too good to pass up. Besides, by giving it directly to Max she'd be certain the evidence would be processed quickly.

Scanning the small diner she started to feel a bit less vulnerable. If the man who had just left truly had been the one who'd been dogging her, she could identify him. That was good, and bad. Now that he had revealed himself to her, he had nothing more to lose.

Max and Harper parked half a block from Penny Potter's rented house on the outskirts of Billings and donned black Kevlar vests with FBI printed front and back in big white letters. They had considered approaching the house posing as friendly new neighbors but decided against it. The Potter woman would be more likely to cooperate with easily identifiable agents.

Speaking into the mic clipped to his shoulder, Max gave the standby order. "Harper and I will go in first with the dogs. Everybody hold your positions until I give the order to approach. We don't want to scare a possible victim or give anybody advance warning. Leo, you and Ian cover the rear."

As soon as his teammates had radioed confirmation they were in place, he tightened Opal's leash and started toward the unassuming home. The residential street was normally quiet. With both ends blockaded by Billings police cars it looked totally deserted.

The cell phone in his pocket vibrated. Max ignored it. *Almost there.* "I'll go first so Opal can clear the way, then you follow. Keep your eyes open but no guns. Use Star for apprehension if need be. There's supposed to be a little boy in here."

"Affirmative. We've had surveillance in place for the past twenty-four hours. There's been no sign of the resident. Or of Jake."

"That doesn't mean he's not here." Max raised a fist to knock on the door. "Penny Potter. Open up. FBI."

There was no answer. He announced himself again, then prepared to kick the door in. His hand gripped the knob. It turned.

"Front door is unlocked," Max radioed. "Making entry to check resident welfare. Stand by."

Opal and Max led the way with Agent Prentiss waiting in the doorway. He was always on high alert when his dog was searching for explosives. This time, every nerve in his body was firing. If their intelligence was accurate, this place had ties to Morrow's family and was also within cell tower range of the anonymous tips from someone who might be close to the Duprees. Anything that even hinted of the infamous crime family was bad news, particularly since they had admitted to beginning that series of bombings in retaliation for Reginald's arrest.

Nose to the floor, Opal followed an instinctive pattern, disturbed only when Max told her to recheck certain areas, like closets and the toy chest he found in a tiny room that had obviously housed a child.

Every shadow could hide death, every doorway an armed attacker. Had he not relied on his K-9 partner, his progress would have been considerably slower. And more nerve-wracking. It was bad enough as it was, even though Opal acted as if they were playing a wonderful game of hide-and-seek.

They came to the outdated kitchen. A booster seat was balanced on one of the padded chairs at the worn-out table. The floor was scuffed but nevertheless clean. A few dirty dishes remained in the sink; a used frying pan atop the stove. Max opened the cupboards just to be sure. Opal's response assured him there was no bomb.

"All units, approach with caution. The house

is clear. No sign of the mother or child but we haven't checked the backyard or garage yet."

A volley of "Copy" came back to him. Harper was at his side in seconds. "Star isn't alerting to anything in here, either. I think our chickens have flown the coop."

"Apparently. We need to check for signs of the male occupant the neighbors reported."

"Copy," Harper said. She sniffed and furrowed her brow. Her big shepherd was straining at the short lead. "Do you smell that?"

"Smell what?"

"Expensive aftershave. It reminds me of the way Jake used to smell when he kept leaning over my desk and making passes at me."

Max pointed. "The bathroom is that way. Check it first while I do a sweep of the yard."

He hadn't reached the back porch when he heard Harper shout. "Max! In here."

This time he passed Opal. "What is it?"

"A razor, comb and a bottle of that cologne Jake loved." She pointed to a tiny spot of shaving cream on the sink. "This is still wet!"

Max immediately reached for his radio as he headed for the back door with his dog. "Male occupant may be in the area. Use caution."

Opal's nails clicked on the hard floor as she scrambled to keep pace with her partner. He jerked open the kitchen door and burst out. A high board fence enclosed a small yard. Overgrown bushes filled the corners, some abutting the house. He could see flashing lights of patrol cars in the drive on one side. The other looked open.

"Prentiss, backyard. All other units stand by."

Harper appeared immediately, her German shepherd at her side. Max signaled for her to circle wider into the unencumbered grass while he stayed next to the building. He used Opal to warn them of any booby traps. There was no time for a slower, more meticulous search—not if their quarry was getting away.

One realization bothered Max. A lot. Whoever had been with the Potter woman was acting almost as savvy and capable as a trained agent. Taking him into custody was not going to be easy.

Farther out on the lawn, opposite the corner of the house Max was approaching, Harper held Star on a short lead. Max gave her a hand signal to proceed and they coordinated their movements without speaking.

Opal lunged. Star's deep bark echoed off the house and fence. For a split second Max saw a tall, lanky, dark-haired man slip around a corner and disappear.

Harper shouted, "Is that him?"

Both agents were running at top speed. The dogs would have been faster off leash but they didn't dare release them until they were sure of their target.

Max started to reply, "Looked like him," when his words were drowned out by the rev of a motorcycle engine. Tires squealed. Max rounded the corner just in time to see someone speeding off. When the rider turned to look back he was grinning and wearing the mirrored sunglasses typical of federal agents. If Jake had dyed his dirty-blond hair the resemblance would be uncanny.

"Person of interest fleeing west on a motorbike. Possibly red. No helmet. May be armed and dangerous." Sirens in the distance told him there were cars in pursuit.

He turned back to Agent Prentiss. "Bag those clues in the bathroom while Opal and I check the garage, just to be safe."

"Yes, sir."

The cell phone in Max's pocket buzzed again. This time he answered. "West." The moment the caller spoke his already fast pulse shot off the charts.

Katerina sounded breathless. "I saw him. I mean I met him. He came into the diner—"

"Who did?"

"The guy who's been stalking me. I thought he looked a little familiar when I served him but I wasn't sure until he said something."

"Then you can identify him? What's his name?"

"He said it was Kyle."

"No last name?" Max clenched his teeth. He needed to be there, to look after Katerina. Identifying her stalker face-to-face put her in far more jeopardy than before.

"He didn't say. But I got you something better. I have his prints on his coffee mug."

"Great! Is he still there?"

"No. He left right after I told him about the explosion at the ranch." Max heard her catch her breath. "Oh, and he told me what he's looking for. You aren't going to believe this. He said Vern hid diamonds!"

"What?"

"You heard me. Diamonds. I have no idea where he got them or why he hid them but that's what Kyle is looking for. He thinks Vern told me where they are."

Pausing, Max considered waiting to ask his next question until they were together again, then changed his mind. "*Did* he tell you?"

"Of course not!" Katerina was practically shouting into the phone.

"I had to ask. I hope you understand. I wouldn't be doing my job if I didn't."

Her "Fine" was crisp and her mood hard to interpret.

"Where are you now?"

"Still at work," she said. "I stepped out into the alley to call you so we wouldn't be overheard."

Max checked the time. "Okay. It's going to take me hours to wrap up here and make it back to you. Promise you'll be careful, Katerina. Stay around people. Don't be caught alone unless you're locked in a room at the hotel."

"What shall I do with the fingerprints?"

"Put the mug into a plastic bag and try to keep it from rubbing on the sides. We may get DNA from where the guy drank, too."

"Okay. I promised my boss that I'd work a double shift. I'll stay here until morning unless you come to get me before that."

"Fine. I'll send someone by to pick up the mug so it doesn't get misplaced. Just hang on to it until then."

"Gotcha. How's your investigation going up there?"

"Don't ask," Max said. "Just take care of yourself."

"I…" Her words were cut off by a vibration and boom that was so loud it hurt his ear.

"*Katerina!* Katerina, answer me. What just happened?"

She didn't have to reply for him to know. There had been another explosion in California.

And this time he wasn't there to pick up the pieces.

Or Katerina Garwood.

TEN

The blast rocked Katerina's world, its flash nearly blinding her despite the bright summer sun that beat down. Instinct caused her to drop the cell phone, duck and cover her head. In the background she began to hear shouting and wailing. Shards of the diner's plate-glass windows lay in the street. Its Miner's Grub sign was hanging by one wire, swinging like a bird's broken wing and looking so pitiful she wanted to cry.

A brief mental check of her own physical condition proved she was uninjured, so she straightened and picked her way back inside. The dining area was in shambles. Broken glass and crockery lay scattered on every flat surface. Exterior windows were missing. Seats from a rear booth were shredded like confetti while the table had been upended and lay in the aisle.

She shouted to her boss. "Xavier, are you okay?"

His "Aye, aye, aye, what happened?" echoed from the kitchen.

"I think it was a bomb," she answered. "Come help me if you can. And call 9-1-1. My phone is broken."

The middle-aged man pushed his way out of the kitchen and surveyed the ruins of his diner. A phone was pressed to one ear and he had tears in his eyes. "They want to know if anybody is hurt," he relayed to Katerina as she tended to an elderly woman with a napkin pressed to her shoulder.

"We didn't have many customers but some do have cuts from the flying glass. They'd better send ambulances."

Firemen in turnouts were first through the opening where the door used to hang. They triaged victims and organized their treatment while uniformed officers tried to get answers. Katerina recognized Sheriff Tate, who was the first to approach her.

Instead of offering sympathy or asking if she was all right, he gestured to one of the patrolmen. "Arrest this young woman until we get everything sorted out," he said, taking Katerina's arm and pulling her away from the victim she'd been comforting. "She was involved in another bombing a few days ago."

"This is not my fault!" Katerina resisted being manhandled and jerked out of his grasp. "Ask the FBI. They'll tell you I'm innocent."

"I don't see any FBI agents," the sheriff said

with a mock grin. Handing her over to the police he backed off and dusted his hands together as if removing dirt. "Far as I'm concerned you can keep that girl locked up till she confesses."

"To what?" Katerina shouted.

"Conspiracy to commit murder. I'm sure we can come up with a few other charges but that one'll hold you for now."

Incredulous, she scanned the crowd looking for anyone who would stand up for her. Most seemed to be in shock, although a few were nodding as if they agreed with her accuser. Even Xavier made no move to interfere in her arrest.

Call Max, her mind screamed. But she couldn't. Not only was the cell phone he'd given her lying in the alley with a cracked screen, she had failed to memorize his private number because there had been no need.

He'll come for me, she told herself over and over. He had to have overheard the blast while they'd been talking and would certainly realize she needed his help. Besides, he was trying to track down associates of the Duprees and one of their trademarks had been bombings. Max would be back.

As she was dragged through what was left of the front door, Katerina remembered the clue she'd preserved. She looked back. Everything had been blown off the prep counter. Including the mug with the evidence. Even if she managed to locate the right one in the rubble there would be no way to prove it was Kyle's and check his prints.

The bad guys had won. Again.

Max arranged for an FBI helicopter to pick him up and fly him to an airport. No commercial flight for him this time. He'd insisted on a government jet and got it. By the time he landed and picked up his SUV, barely three hours had elapsed.

Communications with Dylan O'Leary brought him up to speed on the diner explosion as he drove south. Injuries were, thankfully, minor. Because Katerina had been outside talking to him when the bomb went off, she had escaped completely.

"Except that they arrested her," Dylan added grimly.

"*What?* On what charge?"

"You're gonna get a kick out of this. Attempted murder. My sources tell me she was held because the sheriff insisted. They also tell me that particular lawman is a close friend of her daddy's."

"Bertrand Garwood again," Max gritted out. "I'm beginning to see him as a link rather than Katerina."

Dylan chuckled. "Is that because he's not as pretty as his daughter?"

"Hah. Very funny, although true. Her mother

must have been a real stunner because she sure doesn't look like her dad."

"I take it that's a plus," the techie said.

"Oh, yeah." Max kept his eyes on the road while his mind took a detour. Visualizing Katerina being put in handcuffs and hauled off to jail was intolerable. How scared she must be. The mere thought of tears pooling in those beautiful, expressive blue eyes pierced his gut like a lance and made him yearn to take her in his arms and assure her that everything was going to be okay. He'd see to it. Somehow.

"Headquarters to Special Agent West," Dylan quipped. "Did you hear what I said?"

"Yeah, but I didn't like it."

"Well, chill. Your girlfriend is safer locked up in a local jail than she'd be on the street right now."

Max exhaled a long, deep breath. "As much as I hate to admit it, I suppose I agree. Have you run across any new threats?"

"A few. That sheriff owes her plenty considering the way he spoke out and blamed her in front of all those bystanders and first responders. It's going to take a while to convince some folks she had nothing to do with the bombing."

"Do you think someone was trying to get her?"

To Max's relief, Dylan said, "No. If they had

been they wouldn't have waited until she was outside before triggering the device."

"Unless it was random and they weren't watching."

"There is that. How far out are you?"

"An hour, give or take. I'm using my lights but no siren."

"This is an emergency?"

Max snorted before answering, "It is to me."

The Mariposa County Jail wasn't all that bad if Katerina compared it to her former apartment, particularly after Kyle had trashed it. At least there was a cot and a blanket and pillow in her cell.

Waiting for Max would have been intolerable if she had not expended so much nervous energy after the blast. As the jolt of adrenaline began to wear off, her body responded with core-deep weariness.

Although she promised herself she'd stay awake and try to figure out who could have planted the explosive device in poor Señor Alvarez's little diner, her body insisted she must rest. That's why she lay down on the cot. And why she was awakened by Max's voice several hours later.

"Katerina! Are you all right?"

Her lids fluttered open in time to watch him demand that the cell door be unlocked. The sight of him brought instantly renewed hope and strength, both of which were sorely needed.

She swung her legs over the side of the cot and sat up. Words were inadequate to express her feelings at that moment. Max was here. He'd come back. She started to stand, wobbled a tiny bit and felt him lift her into his embrace.

Never had she felt so safe. Her arms slipped around his waist and she held tight. "Oh, Max, they blew up the diner. It was awful." Katerina felt his warm breath on her hair and wondered if she was imagining the rain of kisses, the press of his lips. Tightening her hold she whispered, "I'm so glad you're here."

She heard a catch in his throat when he asked, "Are you sure you're all right?"

"I am now."

"Reports say nobody was killed or badly injured. Is that what you saw?" His hold on her remained firm.

"Yes." After several long moments she raised her face to gaze at him and was rewarded with the soft brush of his lips on hers.

"I nearly died when I heard that blast and you stopped talking."

"I dropped the phone you gave me. It broke. I didn't have your number written down." She glanced to one side. "Tate thinks I'm some kind of mad bomber."

"So I heard." Max began to smile with tenderness. "He may not realize it but he did us a favor. You were far safer waiting for me in this cell than you would have been going back to your hotel room."

"Can you get me out?"

"Already done," he said huskily. "You're now officially in federal custody. Ready to go?"

Katerina kept one arm around his waist and he encircled her shoulders as they turned and left together. Wondering what she would have done, how she could have coped without Max's help made her tremble. There was no way she could deny how desperately she needed him, nor did she want to. It wasn't weakness to acknowledge a need for moral support, it was a matter of setting aside foolish pride and admitting she wasn't as complete as she had imagined.

Oh, she had her faith and believed Jesus was with her in all things, yet there was also an instinctive desire for an earthly friend who would stand by her. Defend her when she was attacked or falsely accused. Just be there.

That was where Max came in. His presence filled her with a sense of strength and rightness that had been missing for as long as she could remember. As she mulled over recent events she was amazed at how, despite efforts to harm her and those she loved, God had turned evil into good.

There were still plenty of serious hurdles to overcome, of course, but Max had returned without her asking. And he had sought her out, made arrangements to help her, stood by her even after admitting he'd had doubts about her innocence.

And now, finally, she could help him with his investigation. The fingerprints on the mug were gone, yes, but her memory remained sharp. She could identify the cohort of her late fiancé and give Max something to work with that might tie to others and snowball into solving the entire case.

Then there were the diamonds, assuming Vern hadn't lied about that, too. It was a possibility. After all, if he was being pressed to deliver drugs or money and didn't have it, he might have invented a story about hiding gemstones just to save his own neck.

Which hadn't worked, she thought, realizing that her initial notion about why he'd died may have been right. If he'd been tortured too much and had kept holding back because he had no choice, he could very easily have driven his tormentors to press him too hard. Dead was dead, of course. It just seemed more logical to assume they had not meant to kill Vern until they'd made him talk.

Once in the street, she paused and looked up at Max. "What if nobody finds any diamonds? What if they don't even exist?"

"One day at a time, honey," he said gently. "I want to get you back to the hotel where we can talk privately and try to sort out the facts as we know them."

Blinking back tears, Katerina never took her eyes off him when she said, "The only thing I know for sure is that I have never been so happy to see anybody as I am to see you."

"Likewise, Ms. Garwood. When I heard that blast over the phone I couldn't stop thinking…"

"Yeah. Me, too. If I'd been clearing off that table instead of calling you, I might have been blown up."

"Can you describe the last customer who was sitting in the booth at the heart of the damage?"

Slowly, thoughtfully, she shook her head. "It's all a blur. The whole afternoon is. I'm sorry."

"Don't worry about it. I have a few tricks we can try to jog your memory. They sometimes help a lot."

"Sometimes?"

Max nodded. "Yes. If one thing doesn't work we try others. My job isn't pure science the way they depict it on TV. It's more like throwing mud at a wall and hoping some of it will stick. Speaking of mud, did you get your prize ribbons clean?"

"Yes. Thanks for asking. They aren't as pretty as they once were but they'll do as mementos."

"I'm glad," Max said softly.

Katerina knew he meant it from the bottom of his heart. Although they had known each other for a very short time, she was already able to read him like a book. For the most part, anyway. No doubt he was hiding parts of his psyche that he felt were too vulnerable to reveal but she could wait. It was enough to know that he cared, to see the tenderness in his gaze and feel the tingle his deep voice brought on when they were speaking privately. The depth and scope of those feelings were new to her. Overwhelming. What was the most unsettling was an assuredness that Vern had never affected her that way. Not even when he'd proposed. Perhaps that was why she had hesitated before agreeing to marry him.

She let Max help her into the car before she closed her eyes and whispered, "Thank You, God, for interfering before I made the second biggest mistake of my life." And speaking of life... "Thank You for preserving mine and keeping the customers safe."

Katerina's subconscious continued the prayer silently as Max slid behind the wheel. Just looking at him made her so thankful it brought tears to her eyes. She dashed them away so he wouldn't notice.

There was no place she'd rather be than right there. And nobody she'd rather be sitting beside. The threatening world outside the SUV no longer terrified her as long as her handsome special agent was nearby.

"You okay?" Max asked as they drove toward the hotel.

"Fine. More than fine," Katerina said, taking the chance that he shared her feelings. "You're here."

Max had to wait for his heart to slow down before he dared try small talk. He had not intended to make Katerina dependent upon him, it had just happened. In this case it was probably beneficial since he did want her compliance and cooperation. He hoped that she understood he was not actually courting her, he was simply doing his job—at least that was what he kept telling himself when his emotions took over.

He chanced a sidelong glance beneath arched eyebrows. "Thanks. Our FBI motto is Fidelity, Bravery, Integrity."

"Nice. I read it on the seal."

"It's not just a pretty logo. It's how we live our lives, Katerina," Max told her.

"So..." She deftly switched gears. "How did everything turn out with the missing agent you were searching for back in Montana?"

"Not sure. We spotted someone who looked a little like him fleeing the scene, but until we get some DNA results back we're just guessing."

"What happened to that poor woman and her baby?"

He saw no reason to withhold information that was no longer classified since they'd used local Billings police in the raid. "Long gone. She may have fled for any number of reasons."

"What do you think?"

"All I know for sure is that I saw a person of interest ride off on a motorbike and he escaped. The only thing that actually ties him to that particular house is who had been living there."

"Even your specially trained dogs couldn't track him?"

Max frowned. "No. The man apparently had an escape plan. The question is, why was he still there when Penny Potter and the child were gone? It was almost as if he was taunting us."

"Maybe he just came looking for them after they were already on the run and he was trying to figure out where they had gone."

"I suppose that is possible."

Katerina grew thoughtful. "What would be this mystery man's reason for taunting you if he didn't know who you and your team were?"

"Are you suggesting he may have really been Jake?"

"I don't know. I don't know the guy. It was just a theory.

"No way. He would have reported to the FBI as

soon as he managed to escape from his kidnappers and have asked fellow agents for assistance."

"Fidelity."

"And integrity," Max added. "Jake Morrow has always been something of a loose cannon but he was—is—an excellent agent. He and his younger half brother, Zeke, weren't raised together but Zeke followed him into the FBI. They're both products of dysfunctional families."

"A person isn't necessarily locked in to a personality flaw forever," Katerina agreed softly. "I have high hopes to escape from the kind of prejudice I listened to most of my life. Now that I recognize it, I should be able to put it behind me."

His lips quirked. "You? Flaws?"

"Don't tease. I mean it. I never knew what a stuck-up snob I was until I got to see the world from the other side."

"So, your enemies did you a favor."

"I guess they did." She began to smile again. "We'll see if it was all worth it after the dust settles."

"I come from a big family," Max said. "We all get along pretty well, considering. I suppose it was hard for you, being an only child, after your mother passed away."

When Katerina looked over at him and he saw the glisten of unshed tears he realized he'd touched a nerve. "It was the worst time of my life.

And the best. The loneliness and alienation from my dad pushed me to spend more and more time training horses. If I'd been happy and fulfilled already I might never have become so proficient."

"Pressure turns coal into diamonds," Max observed. "You don't suppose that was what Kowalski meant when he said he had diamonds, do you?"

"Not for a second. He was a crook. He stole from his bosses and paid the ultimate price. I didn't figure into the equation."

"Then we have some work to do," he said soberly.

"I like the way that sounds. The two of us. Together."

"Absolutely." There was no way he was letting Katerina out of his sight if he could help it. As long as his assignment could be made to justify it, he intended to keep her so close she'd probably get claustrophobia.

"Together." Max grinned. "Just you, me and Opal."

ELEVEN

With a weather forecast of bright, clear skies and no hint of impending storms for a least two weeks, the South Fork Chamber of Commerce decided to announce the rescheduling of its Founder's Day picnic and parade. Considering the crime wave she'd been experiencing, Katerina was more concerned about that kind of activity than she was the weather.

"Are we going to visit the ranch again and look for diamonds?" she asked Max over the breakfast provided by the hotel the following morning.

"Yes, why?"

"Because I'd like you to try to talk some sense into my father."

Max chuckled. "You think that highly of my powers of persuasion? I'm flattered."

"Well, he won't even speak to me. He might listen to a man in authority."

"Do you want me to defend your actions and

explain that you didn't have anything to do with the bombs?"

Katerina shook her head. "No. I want you to convince him that it's too dangerous for him to participate in the Founder's Day festivities. Particularly riding in the parade in an open car."

"What makes you think he's in danger?"

"Everything. Look at what's happened so far. His stable was blown up, then my apartment was trashed. The awful bombing at the Miner's Grub should convince him of something."

"Not if he assumes it's all tied to you."

"There's more," Katerina said. "It just came to me. When that guy was threatening me at work he mentioned my family. Dad's all I have left."

"You care about him. I get that." Max sighed. "Okay. I'll give it a try. What do you say we take a ride out that way today?"

"You're free?" The instant those words were out of her mouth she likened them to the humorous reply, *No, but I'm reasonable*, and began to blush.

Max noticed immediately. "What's wrong?"

"Nothing. My mind just works in strange ways."

"I've noticed," he said teasingly. "Sometimes you're so far ahead of me it's scary."

"Really?"

"Really. You aced all your classes in school, didn't you?"

Her cheeks felt even warmer. "Yes. At the time I thought I was chasing 4.0 to impress my father but in retrospect I can see it was a matter of personal pride." She sobered. "I hope that's not a sin."

Max laughed. "You are unbelievable. Think about it this way. If you slacked off and didn't do your best, you'd be wasting God-given talent. Isn't that worse?"

"You're right!"

"Always," he quipped. "Now finish your toast and let's get a move on."

Katerina sipped cooling coffee, then blotted her lips with a napkin. "I'm ready when you are. I just wish there was something I could do for Señor Alvarez. He's lost everything thanks to me."

"Stop blaming yourself. If his insurance comes up short I may be able to get him some help from a victims' reparations fund. I heard that the restaurant kitchen is still intact. If he can rebuild the dining room he should be back in business in no time."

Her hand rested at the base of her throat and she fought tears of relief. "Oh, thank God. Literally."

"You've been praying for your boss, too?"

Releasing a quavering breath, she nodded. "Of course I have. And for all the people who were hurt by the debris. That's the easy part."

"There's a hard part about praying?" Max looked confused.

"Oh, yes," Katerina replied solemnly. "It's much harder to make myself pray for my enemies and others who have hurt my feelings or given up on me."

"You really do that?"

"When I can manage to get myself into the right frame of mind for long enough, I do. It's one thing to know I should forgive and another thing to actually accomplish it."

Max's jaw clenched. "So, you think guys like the Duprees, who have ruined countless lives, should be forgiven? That's crazy."

She was shaking her head. "I don't mean that anybody should be free of the consequences of their actions, good or bad. Lawbreakers have to pay. Vern Kowalski paid the ultimate price for his sins. But if I harbor anger and hate in my heart, the only one who suffers is me. Take my father for instance."

"Because he's so mad at you?" Max was rising. Opal stood leashed and ready at his side.

"No," Katerina said. "I've been giving it a lot of thought and I've come to the conclusion Dad is furious with God for taking my mother from him. I'm just collateral damage."

"Very perceptive. And possibly true. Not that there's much you can do about it."

"I know." She pushed back her chair and joined

him. "Which is why I'm so thankful for you. I needed an ally and now I have one."

"You must have some local friends who haven't totally abandoned you."

"A few. The time I spent with Vern alienated a lot of them. Besides, they have families and other worries. The last thing I want to do is expose them to the threats that are piling up around me." She smiled and took his free arm. "You, on the other hand, are armed and dangerous. God knew just what I needed."

Her opinion amused Max at first. He had never been called heaven-sent before. Most of the people he encountered who were not part of his team or in other branches of law enforcement treated him with disdain or distrust or both.

"Thanks, I think," he said gruffly, leading the way outside. "But remember, I'm only here temporarily. I could be recalled at any time."

"I understand."

He didn't think she did. Not in the least. She had identified him as a personal answer to her prayers and was going to be devastated when he left. Which he would definitely do. What did she expect? How could she possibly see a positive outcome when his goal had to be to wrap up his current assignment and go back to Montana?

"I will leave, Katerina. It's inevitable."

"I know."

What could she be thinking? Yes, she was an attractive woman and yes, they had grown closer than he got with most of the civilians he met, but that didn't mean he saw a future for them together. There was only one thing to do. He had to put it into words that would make her understand.

"I have a duty to perform. That's why I'm here. It's my job."

The quizzical look on her face told him she was not yet following his line of reasoning.

"My actions and decisions are based on the case I'm working. In this instance it's about the Dupree crime family and their network of underlings. That's why I came to see you. I needed to delve into your relationship with Kowalski and make sure you weren't working with him."

"Okay. And…?"

It was clearly time to get more specific. "And, my job is very dangerous. I could get shot." He hesitated, then plunged ahead. "Plus, I am way too old for you."

To Max's chagrin Katerina began to laugh. He scowled. "What's so funny?"

"You are," she said between giggles. "I wasn't making a pass at you. I was just stating my faith."

"That's not how it sounded."

When her gaze rose to meet his, Max saw pathos in her expression, something he had not expected.

"Are you a believer?" she asked.

"I used to go to church if that's what you mean."

"Not at all." She was slowly shaking her head. "Was there ever a time when you knew, just knew, that God loved you and Jesus did, too?"

Remaining silent, he refused to answer. His subconscious, however, caused his free hand to rise and trace the scar on his cheek.

"How did you get that?" Katerina asked softly. "Was that when your faith was tested and you let it go?"

"That's no concern of yours."

"Yes, it is," she countered, stepping closer and gently cupping his cheek. The touch was barely there, yet it reached all the way into his heart.

Max stopped her by grabbing her wrist and holding tight. "Don't."

She looked up at him, her eyes glistening. "I'm sorry. For a lot of reasons. I wish there was some way I could prove that God never gives up on a believer. He's still here, still caring for you, whether you know it or not."

"That doesn't matter. What happened, happened. Nobody can change the past."

"No, but you can change the way you view it, your reactions to it." Her gaze never wavered. "Look what simmering anger has done to my father."

"It's not the same thing."

"Isn't it?" Katerina stepped back and Max released her wrist.

"No. It isn't," he said flatly. "I got this scar when I failed to accurately profile a supposedly reformed father. A drug lord assumed that man was a snitch and finished him by blowing up his house. My error cost the lives of everybody in the family, including the little boy I had promised to help."

"Oh, Max. How horrible."

Turning away, he shook off the comment rather than reply. *Horrible* didn't begin to cover the feelings he'd had when he'd come to after the explosion and seen the destruction all around him. The scar on his cheek was nothing compared to the loss of life.

As he escorted Katerina to his SUV and put Opal in first, he bit out, "Where was God *then*?"

"Right beside you," she said with tenderness. "I can't begin to explain why bad things happen, I only know I'd be lost without my faith. That's what faith is, sticking with your belief in spite of not knowing. I don't have to be able to explain things on an earthly plane in order to trust God. It's a personal decision."

She paused while he circled the SUV and slid behind the wheel, then continued, "I also believe that once you have turned to Jesus He won't let you go. Even if you give up on Him, He'll stick with you."

He wished he could agree with her theology. His mind didn't work that way. He needed proof and as far as he was concerned, the untimely death of an innocent little boy was a deal breaker. If God wanted his renewed allegiance, He was going to have to do more than send a starry-eyed young woman to preach to him.

A lot more.

Katerina spent the drive to the Garwood Ranch in silent contemplation and prayer. She was no pastor, no Bible scholar. Explaining her faith was something she'd never been asked to do before and she felt woefully ill equipped. What should she have said? What might she add that would help Max get over his heartache and realize how valuable his skills were?

As he wheeled under the archway she realized she was out of time to speak to him in private. *Father, help me say the right thing, the healing thing. Please? I'm way out of my depth here.*

She took a deep breath and plunged ahead. "You're being too hard on yourself, Max. When you're doing your best, when you're following your calling, all anybody expects is the best you can do. Nobody's perfect."

"I agree. Lots of people fail. The trouble is, when I made a mistake, people died. A child died."

What else could she say? How could she argue that point? He was right, as far as he'd gone. But there was more to it. There had to be. Life might appear random, yet be following a master plan. If the physical world did not operate systematically it would disintegrate. The same was true of human existence.

She decided to try one more time. "Look, I don't have all the answers any more than you do. Evil exists. The same rules that govern the universe apply down here. Think of cause and effect. Consequences are a given. They may vary but they won't vanish like some kind of celestial magic trick. God doesn't break the rules on a whim. But he did give us the Bible for direction and understanding."

"You understand it all?"

She had to smile. "Oh, no. I barely get the simple concepts. If the Lord had spelled out everything for us it wouldn't have helped, either. Our minds are incapable of rising to that level of comprehension. Again, that's where faith comes in. And free will. You either choose to believe or you reject that teaching."

Max had turned away to concentrate on Opal. When he looked back at Katerina she could tell their conversation about spirituality was over. That was actually a big relief to her.

He motioned. "You coming with me?"

"Do I have to?"

"You do," he said with a wry smile. "If I have to face the mayor of South Fork and warn him to call off his parade, you need to be there to back me up. After all, you've been the victim of two explosions."

"Don't remind me." Although she did keep pace with Opal and her partner, she took care to avoid leading the way. Despite the fact that she was courageous and confident, standing at a door and knowing her father was going to be the one to open it unnerved her. She didn't fear him, per se. She merely disliked conflict—and Bertrand Garwood was conflict personified.

When they were all three on the porch, Max rang the bell. Katerina stood her ground in spite of a growing desire to escape to the solitude and safety of the remaining stables. Nobody answered the door.

"Do you intend to put Opal to work again while we're here?" Katerina asked as they waited.

"Might as well. I figured you and I could inspect the barns together after Opal tells me they're safe. That okay with you?"

"Fine." She didn't realize she was wringing her hands until Max looked pointedly at them.

"You nervous?"

"No more than I would be if I were empty-handed and locked in a stall with a mean wild mustang."

"Want to go to the tack room and get a whip?"

"A quirt. That's the little whip a rider holds. It makes noise when you smack the business end and works more to get a horse's attention than to hurt him."

"I doubt we'll have trouble getting your dad's attention," Max said as he pushed the doorbell again. "The problem may be in getting him to ignore us while we conduct a serious search."

Before Katerina had a chance to answer, the object of her worry jerked open the heavy wooden door and bellowed, "What now?"

"Special Agent West," Max said, offering a handshake rather than flashing his badge. "We met when—"

"I know when we met." Bertrand scowled. "Why are you here?"

"A couple of reasons, Mr. Garwood. I understand you're scheduled to ride in a parade this coming weekend. That may be inadvisable."

"What's it to the FBI?"

"Concern for your safety, sir."

"Bah!" He gestured at Katerina. "She put you up to this, didn't she?"

"No, sir. There was another bomb set off in town. Surely you heard about it."

"I heard," the portly older man said. When he looked at Katerina again his expression was unreadable.

"Then you understand why I'm suggesting you keep a lower profile."

"I have friends in the sheriff's department. They'll take care of me."

"Still, since your daughter has apparently been targeted twice, it would be wise to take precautions."

Katerina could almost hear her father's reply before he said, "That has nothing to do with me. Everybody knows I have no daughter," then slammed the door.

That attitude was no surprise to Katerina. It did, however, send her emotions spinning.

"I'm so sorry," Max said. He slipped an arm around her shoulders and gave her a supportive squeeze. "I'll contact Tate personally and fill him in, just in case your father is lying about having proper protection lined up for the whole day."

"Thanks." She was shaking her head and sighed audibly. "Remember what I said about needing to forgive him? Well, it's getting harder and harder to do."

"Good to know you're human," Max said gently. "Come on. Let's make a sweep of the barns with Opal while you look for good hiding places for those diamonds."

Katerina rolled her eyes. "I don't know where to start. I mean, every bale of hay, every sack of grain, every stall is a possibility."

"Not necessarily."

"What do you mean?" She was having to take two steps for every stride of his to keep up.

"The places you just mentioned all have drawbacks. Hay and grain can be fed. Stalls are raked and cleaned out regularly. They're not secure enough."

"So, it needs to be someplace stationary?"

"That's more likely. Even the trucks and trailers are an iffy choice. Suppose your father sold one or shipped it away with horses in it? Then how would Vern have retrieved his stash?"

She brightened. "You're right! And when we find the diamonds you can announce it and get that terrible stalker off my trail."

"That would be the ideal result," Max said pensively.

Katerina saw doubt in his expression. "You don't think it will help?"

"It's not that. My concern is based on what I know of the Dupree crime family. They don't let traitors like Kowalski get away with stealing from them."

"*They* had him killed? I assumed it was some

other prisoner who'd heard about the diamonds and wanted to cut himself in."

"It may have been, if Vern was dumb enough to brag, but I doubt it." Max kept working Opal along the edges of the barns as they talked. "Latest word on the street is that Angus Dupree, the uncle of the kingpin we arrested, had already offered an enormous reward to anyone who could get the truth out of your old boyfriend. Once he heard about the gemstones, he was livid. He'd like the loot found and returned, of course, but he doesn't care about the monetary value nearly as much as he does the Dupree reputation."

"But—"

"Let me finish." He paused and faced her. "Pride governs his actions. Pride and a need for retribution. He can no longer count on making Kowalski pay for his crimes against the family. Do you see what I'm saying?"

Nodding, Katerina felt the strength flowing out of her. Vern was gone. There was only one other connection. One other person who could be punished to bring him satisfaction.

Her.

TWELVE

Failing to get any leads that day, Max brought in Zeke Morrow and his tracking dog, an Australian shepherd named Cheetah, just in case Vern had wrapped the diamonds in something personal of his before hiding them. They got clothing samples from the jail and picked up a waiting warrant for the ranch.

After a thorough search that included the main house, Zeke reported to Max. "Nothing, Boss. Sorry. Even if he used a sock or T-shirt it's been too long."

"I figured. I just thought you'd be glad for a break from all that hassle about your half brother."

"Thanks. I was hoping you and Harper would come up with something helpful at Penny Potter's when you were in Billings."

Max nodded. "Yeah, so did I. Any word from the stakeout of her place?"

"No. Nothing. She did a better job of vanishing on her own than the US Marshals did hiding Esme Dupree."

"That reminds me," Max said. "What about Esme? Do we have any leads on her whereabouts?"

"Not that I've heard. I've been in the field quite a bit lately."

"I get regular briefings on my computer and smartphone," Max said. "I wondered about rumors."

"It's been quiet. They did tell you about the anonymous text messages, didn't they?"

"Messages? Plural? I know about the one we got right before we raided Penny Potter's."

"There were two more after that. The first said something like, 'Nah, nah, you missed him.' The second was even harder to understand. We finally decided they had to be GPS coordinates but they didn't pan out. Led us to a vacant house."

"All right," Max said. "We'll continue to treat the Potter woman as a blameless victim like Esme until we're sure otherwise."

"She really may be innocently caught up in all this, you know."

"I know. That's why we're giving her the benefit of the doubt."

Zeke's dark eyes narrowed on a slim figure in the distance. "What about the Garwood woman?

Are you doing the same for her or are you playing her?"

"She's innocent," Max said firmly. "Dupree bombs have come close to ending her life twice already. There's no way anybody with half a brain would put themselves in dangerous situations like that on purpose."

"If you say so." The other agent arched an eyebrow. "I know how easy it can be for a pretty face to turn an agent."

Ignoring the insinuation, Max asked, "Is that what you think may have happened to your half brother?"

Zeke shrugged. "No, no. But he did seem right on track until he got involved with that Penny woman and fathered her kid." He huffed. "Of course, he and I weren't raised together so it's hard for me to speculate. All I know is I owe him for inspiring me to join the FBI."

Offering his hand, Max shook with the slightly younger agent and wished him well. "Thanks for coming. Have a good flight home."

"Sorry I couldn't be of more help. Are you heading back to headquarters soon, too?"

"Probably. I need to use Opal to check a parade route tomorrow morning, to make sure it isn't booby-trapped. So far there hasn't been any loss of life around here but with a crowd lined up along a narrow street the chances of injury multiply."

Zeke grinned. "I have to say I'm happier chasing crooks and doing search and rescue than I would be following Opal around looking for bombs. I don't know how you do it."

"One careful step at a time." Max mirrored the grin. "It's like being on a dull stakeout and then hearing gunshots. You go from calm to panic in a heartbeat. Most of the time it's hard to keep my edge because we usually come up empty."

"So, do you want to send the Duprees a thank-you note for helping with your training?"

Max laughed. "I think I'll skip that this time."

As far as Katerina was concerned, the search of the ranch was hopeless. She'd poked through the stables until she was sneezing from the dust and had accompanied both federal agents while they used their K-9 partners to canvas her father's house and all the barns. If there really were diamonds hidden there she had no idea where they could be.

Right now, her main worry was her father's safety. Yes, he could be cruel and, yes, she sometimes got so mad at him she could scream, but he was still her daddy. Memories of the way Bertrand had acted during her early childhood sustained and bolstered her. He had loved her once. Surely there had to be a tiny trace of that parental affection left, even if he chose to deny it.

She rode into South Fork with Max and Opal to point out the parade route and suggest places where the biggest crowds would gather.

"They'll march along Main, then turn on Park Street and everybody will head up to the city park for a barbecue. There's no way one dog can police it all, no matter how good Opal is."

The boxer stuck her broad chest between the front bucket seats and gave Katerina a slurp on the cheek. She giggled and wiped at it with the sleeve of her bright pink T-shirt. "Eww. I love you, too."

"That's what you get for mentioning her name when she's not in uniform yet."

"Yeah. You'd think I'd have learned that by now. Doesn't she ever get tired of working? I mean like yesterday morning when you didn't find a thing?"

"She can. If she starts to look bored I sometimes plant the odor of explosives and let her find it so I can reward her."

"That's smart. I can see where she'd love that kind of game. I just wish we didn't have to keep playing it for real." Katerina pointed. "I see that the sheriff and his officers are on duty at the crossroads. If you check the parade route first, they can watch it from then on."

"Affirmative." Max radioed his intentions on a local frequency, then pulled up next to one of the patrol cars. The deputy gave him a high sign that was almost a salute.

"I see you've made peace with Dad's body-guards."

"His friend, Sheriff Tate, is a lot more sensible than Bertrand Garwood. We worked out a cooperative plan. After the parade, Opal and I will stay on scene at the park and circulate to make our presence known, just in case."

"Do you really think there will be more trouble?" The casual atmosphere of the small town seemed so peaceful it was hard to imagine more mayhem—particularly because if it came, it would be because of her.

"Most of my duties are to keep folks safe, not pick up the pieces after a disaster. We can do that, too, we'd just rather head off problems instead."

Main Street was already filling with spectators. Many had brought their own lawn chairs and were staking claim on the best spectator spots along the curb. Katerina ran interference for Opal as she worked the line because so many excited children wanted to rush up and pet her.

"This dog is doing a job now," she explained. "See her vest? When she takes it off you can pet her. Maybe at the picnic, later."

A sweet, red-haired little girl pointed and lisped, "Ith that her name?"

"No. That says FBI. She's like a police officer."

Katerina kept smiling as she watched Max and Opal work their way farther along the street. The boxer's nose was to the ground until she came to a plastic drum that had been placed at a corner to receive extra trash during the celebration.

Max stopped. Opal circled the blue drum once, then sat next to it and panted up at her handler expectantly.

Katerina's heart skipped a beat. That was the sign. Opal had found explosives! And there had to be a dozen innocent little kids close enough to touch both the barrel and the dog.

She saw Max speaking into his radio. Deputies began to converge. Some stayed with Max while others, arms outstretched, began to shoo the crowd away from the corner. Away from possible harm.

"You, too, ma'am," the nearest deputy said. Katerina remembered going to high school with him, but they never really moved in the same circles. "No. I'm with Special Agent West." She pointed to Max. "I have to stay here."

"Orders are to evacuate for half a block. Move along, please." He lowered his voice and leaned closer. "You don't want to start a panic by refusing, do you, Ms. Katerina?"

"Of course not. I…" She had to back up or be overrun. "All right. I'm not going far."

"Down to the sidewalk in front of the hardware

store will be fine," he said pleasantly, as if he had not just warned her of real danger.

From where she and the others stood she watched Max and the sheriff confer. Finally an electric cart built like a small truck was brought in and the blue drum loaded gently into the back.

The driver eased the vehicle forward, inches at a time, while Max led Opal a safe distance away and rewarded her with a favorite chew toy.

Patrol cars, lights flashing, flanked the golf cart as it slowly moved off the parade route. Katerina figured the guy who was driving deserved a medal. She just hoped it didn't end up costing him his life in the process.

Given the choices available in South Fork and the narrow window of opportunity during which the barrel had to have been placed, Max figured it had been delivered with the explosives already inside. That probably meant the device was stable enough to move again rather than wait hours for a bomb squad that might have to travel all the way from San Jose, or farther.

He wasn't thrilled with the sheriff's choice to do so but had to admit it made sense. So did leaving the small cardboard box in the bottom where it lay. Since no other trash had been thrown on top of it since it was left there, he figured that the sooner he checked all the other trash barrels, the better.

They weren't the only places he intended to look, of course. The first thing he'd do was make a circuit of all the blue barrels, then retrace his route and look for other suspicious objects. Hopefully, whoever had booby-trapped the trash receptacle lacked imagination and had simply repeated himself if he'd planted more bombs.

Katerina jogged toward him. Max stopped before Opal reached the fifth barrel. "You need to go wait with the sheriff's deputies."

"You found a bomb already?"

"Opal says we did. It's been taken out of town and left in a safe place, under guard, just in case."

"What if she's wrong?"

Max huffed. "Opal is never wrong. And she never lies. That's another reason why a K-9 partner is better than a human one."

"So, why are you still looking?"

"Because nothing says that whoever put the device in one trash barrel stopped there. With all the confusion surrounding the celebration, it's highly likely there will be more than what I've already located." He didn't like frightening her. It was just that she seemed to be taking the whole situation too lightly. Having been born and raised in a small town had left Katerina too gullible. Too trusting. That mindset had already led her to become involved with a drug smuggler. There was no telling what else she'd have done if the FBI had not sent him to South Fork.

Max gave her his sternest look. "Listen, Katerina. Don't be naive. This is no game. The earlier bombers may have targeted buildings and not cared about an accidental passerby. But the guys who set these bombs wanted to hurt people for sure."

He was relieved to see her shoulders slump and her head nod. "Okay. I'll back off. Can I stay with you and Opal to watch the parade after you're done working? I know there's no way Dad will ever call it off no matter what you find. Not after all this preparation."

What Max should have done, is tell her there was no time during the day when he'd be off duty. Instead, he gave her permission to rejoin him at Main and Park.

Her joyful "All right!" brought a genuine smile.

Max's countenance mirrored her delight. How could a man not be happy when Katerina was around. She was the kind of woman who always saw the glass half-full, the flowers in full bloom, the sun bright in a summer sky. She had been through plenty that should have depressed her, yet she seemed to always bounce back, no matter what life threw at her. Such as her father's rejection. His jaw clenched and anger roiled through him. Garwood had a lot to answer for. He was also a prime target because, no matter how obnoxious he got, he was still related to Katerina.

Max finished checking the last trash barrel and radioed Sheriff Tate with his location. "I've checked and cleared the rest of the route. Did somebody go over the floats and cars?"

"Negative. I've posted a guard but some of them were already parked in the staging area when my man went on duty."

"Copy."

"It's not far from where you are," Tate told Max. "Go past the restrooms and you'll see a bunch of cars and tractors pulling decorated trailers."

"On my way," Max replied. He began to jog, purposely leaving Katerina behind despite minor misgivings. As long as she remained in a crowded area he had already inspected she should be all right. The shops and roads were safe. That left only the rolling stock that could be triggered remotely while passing certain bystanders.

Like Katerina.

Max shivered, picturing the first day he'd seen her a scant few weeks ago. Then, they had not yet formed a bond. Now everything was different. *Very* different if he were to listen to his instincts and put aside arguments against caring for her.

No, that wasn't right, he countered. He might care about her welfare the same way he was concerned for any citizen's well-being. He didn't care *for* her. Because that would mean his feelings were too personal, too special. He didn't want to become romantically involved with any woman, particularly not one who was eleven years younger than he was and tainted by her past.

Max could just hear somebody like Katerina preaching to him about forgiveness and second chances. And she'd be right, up to a point. He had come to believe she was truly innocent. However, that didn't mean his bosses in the FBI would be inclined to trust her, and by association, trust him. Not as totally as they once had, at any rate.

His conscience demanded he take Katerina's side and stand up for her. She was young. That was a given. And she had been terribly spoiled by her father before being ostracized. How awful that must feel. Her whole world had crashed around her, somebody was trying to kill her, the man she had loved had been murdered, and thugs were stalking her for a prize that might never be located.

Pausing, he took a deep breath and visualized Katerina's beautiful eyes and bright smile. Most people would have felt beaten down and have given up, yet she had not. On the contrary, she had bounced back every time, she had opened up to him about her faith. It was solid. Reliable. And by comparison, so was she.

A horn honked. Engines revved. Max saw the procession start to move. Out of time to reach them and inspect each vehicle, he stood aside with Opal and let them slowly pass by. Her stiff posture and intense concentration told him she knew she was still working.

Suddenly she lunged. Barked in spite of her training to remain calm when detecting telltale odors.

Max held up a hand and stepped forward to halt the progress of the antique Packard convertible. Ranch foreman Heath McCabe was driving. Sitting on the rear deck, dressed like a country-western singer, was Bertrand Garwood. He waved Max back. "Out of our way."

"I'm sorry, Mr. Mayor. My dog insists I check your car before you proceed."

"Bah. Ridiculous. Where's my...that young woman who is determined to ruin me?"

"Katerina's not here. And I assure you I am only listening to my detection dog. Now, do you want to let us go over the car the easy way, or do you want to wait for a search warrant and maybe be blown to smithereens in the meantime?"

As Max had figured, the older man spoke to McCabe and had the convertible pulled out of line.

"This won't take long. If you'll both get out, please, I'll let my dog do her job."

Garwood was fuming. "This had better not turn out to be some cooked-up false alarm or I'll have your badge."

If Max had not been so intent on watching Opal he might have laughed. There had been more than one time when he'd have gladly handed over his badge if it had meant he wouldn't have to worry about making another deadly mistake.

"Open the trunk, please."

McCabe took the keys from the ignition and handed them to Max. "Not me, man. I like livin'."

"Are you saying there's an explosive device in the trunk?"

"Nope. But I ain't arguing with your dog, either. If she says it's dangerous, I believe her."

"Actually…" Max led Opal around the idling vehicle one more time. She showed some interest in the trunk but not enough to cause him to call a bomb squad. Using a key he popped the lock and lifted the lid.

"Spare tire, jack, jumper cables…all the usual stuff. Looks like we're okay here."

"What about the undercarriage?" McCabe asked.

"Opal isn't interested in the chassis at all." He started to close the trunk. Opal put her front feet up on the bumper and barked.

Max halted, then picked up the jack handle and used it to gingerly move lightweight items. When he speared a dirty rag and moved it, Opal got very excited.

"This?" he asked, holding it out for her to sniff. The dog went ballistic.

"This? You want this?" Double-checking, he redirected her attention to the car's trunk. She showed zero interest in it. Fixated on the rag she wiggled at his feet.

"Well, well." Max looked to Bertrand. "Where did you get this car, Mr. Garwood?"

"It belongs to me. I only bring it out of storage for parades and such. Why?"

"Because my dog has picked up the odor of an explosive compound on this dirty rag. There's no bomb in your car but somebody who used this rag came in contact with components."

"Well, she's dead wrong. That's the cloth I used this morning to shine the chrome," Bertrand grumbled. "Now, if you're through harassing me, I need to get moving. I'm the parade grand marshal, you know."

Max stepped aside. "Fine by me. Have a nice day."

As the classic Packard pulled away, Max slid the soiled rag into a plastic evidence bag, sealed it and slipped it back in his pocket. If the lab at Quantico could pick out DNA from more than one donor, Garwood might be off the hook. If not, the man had just foolishly admitted to having touched explosives.

Was he vindictive enough to attack his own daughter? Max wondered. He hated to think that but the evidence spoke for itself. Unless there were traces from others on the rag, they may have found their source for at least some of the bombings.

Which brought him back to square one. Components from all but the ranch bomb matched those from other states besides California. Therefore, it was still quite possible that the Duprees' men had bombed the Miner's Grub diner and had probably left the set in the blue trash barrel.

Had Garwood damaged his own stable? The fact that the horses had all been moved out beforehand made it a distinct possibility. But why? Had he known that Katerina was coming back to get her belongings that day?

Max took a deep breath and praised Opal, then put her to work checking all the other floats and cars while he puzzled over the ranch owner's eagerness to admit using the rag. The man wasn't stupid. Why would he incriminate himself when he could have denied knowledge of anything in the trunk? Did he assume law enforcement wouldn't put two and two together? Or was he so sure of his personal connections to the sheriff that he figured he'd never be charged?

That thought settled in the pit of Max's stomach like a sack of placer mine tailings left over from gold mining with water. If he and his team had to arrest Bertrand Garwood, he figured he could quit worrying about his unacceptable feelings for Katerina. She'd never speak to him again.

THIRTEEN

Reluctant to intrude when her father was talking to Max, Katerina waited until he returned to the picnic area with Opal before she approached. "Did you find something odd in Dad's car? I figured it wasn't dangerous when you let him drive on."

"I'm going to send a polishing cloth to the lab to confirm Opal's opinion of it."

"She makes mistakes? I thought trained K-9 cops were infallible."

"Nothing is one hundred percent. It's possible that a solvent in metal polish smells like something Opal's been trained to key in on. The only thing I am sure of is that the little package we found in the bottom of the trash barrel was a bomb. Whether it was set to go off at a certain time or has an electronic detonator is unknown." He released a breath, then went on. "The sheriff didn't want to hold up the festivities so we decided to send it to the town dump and leave it there, under guard. It should be okay until we can get some experts to dismantle it or set it off."

Katerina kept clasping and unclasping her fingers. "This is unbelievable. I mean, no matter what Vern did or didn't do, there's no reason for some distant crime family to target this little town." Wide blue eyes met Max's. "How long is this going to go on? Will we ever get back to normal again?"

She desperately craved solace. Moral support. The sense that someone was there for her. The night that Kyle had entered her hotel room and she'd been so frightened, Max had been her anchor, her comforter. Right now, right here, she was in dire need of a replay.

It seemed wrong to pray for affection so she merely stood still and waited to see what he'd do. Could he sense her neediness? Did he know how disconnected she felt? He must. Whether he was willing to admit it or not, they had an almost tangible emotional connection.

Max stepped near and laid his hand on her arm. "It'll be all right, Katerina. Maybe not today or tomorrow, but things will get better. Trust me. Every time we have an incident and collect more clues we come that much closer to solving this and ending it."

"Do you? The more I learn, the worse it seems."

He moved from the light touch to encircling her

shoulders with his free arm and giving her a quick squeeze. "There are a lot of interconnected crimes and suspects that we have to round up before we'll know enough to totally shut down the Duprees. I imagine you saw on the news that various government agencies formed a task force to break up their organization by arresting the big bosses."

"I remember hearing something like that a few months back. I never dreamed you'd still be chasing them."

"One of the big fish got away. He wasn't first in command but he's bad enough. Angus Dupree is the uncle of Reginald, the head of the organization. Reginald is cooling his heels and awaiting trial along with many of his underlings. We'd love to add his uncle Angus to the docket but he's currently on the run. Unfortunately, so is one of our key witnesses."

"You mean the guy who ran when you were in Billings?

"No, a different one. A woman. The question of who fled from Potter's house should be answered as soon as we get back some results of the DNA samples we gathered from the house.

"What about the mother and baby? Are they all right?"

"We don't know yet. One of my agents, Harper Prentiss, thought she smelled a familiar aftershave in the bathroom at the Potter home but there's nothing positive."

"Oh." Katerina tried to hide her surprise. "Some of your teammates are women?"

"Uh-huh. They make great handlers. A lot of K-9 trainers are female, too."

She knew her cheeks were reddening because they felt awfully warm. "That never crossed my mind."

Leaning closer, Max tilted his head to one side and smiled. "Are you jealous?"

Her "Of course not!" was too quick, too high-pitched to be normal and she could tell from his broadening grin that he knew she was flustered.

"I thought you never lied," Max tsked.

"I don't. I—I…"

He laughed heartily. "I get it. We all tell fibs from time to time to save face or be kind, and don't think anything of it."

"I suppose you're right." Sweeping her hair back from her face with her fingers she tucked it behind her ears. "My, it's hot out today."

"California in the summer. What did you expect?"

Relieved to have been given a plausible reason for her flushed cheeks she agreed. "Right. I hope it's not too hard on Opal. Does she have to wear that vest all day?"

"It's bulletproof," Max explained. "If she did

accidentally set off an explosion the Kevlar might not be enough to save her but it's all the protection I can give her, other than staying out of harm's way as much as possible."

"I suppose K-9 officers do get wounded, just like human ones. I'd never thought of that before. It's sad."

"Any loss of life is."

Judging by the way he had stopped smiling and set his jaw, she realized she'd triggered a painful memory. Curiosity made her ask, "Would you like to talk about it?"

"We already did," Max said curtly.

"Ah, the family with the child. I remember." Forgetting her pride she reached out to him, touched his hand. "Things like that stay with us forever. I know that. I just wish I could give you peace about it."

"You can't."

Gently, lovingly, Katerina said, "I know. Only God can." However, Max had to be willing to accept it, she added to herself. Just as she needed to come to terms with the betrayal of those she loved, Max had to forgive himself—and God. Once, he had trusted his heavenly Father with his life, then had begun to question the turn of events and want to place blame. That was as natural as breathing. And holding a grudge was as destructive as holding his breath. Something had to give or it would do permanent damage.

Gazing into the depths of his piercing blue eyes she sensed a strong connection, as if he were reading her thoughts and knew she was seeing his raw pain, was pulling some of it into her own heart and sharing the struggle.

She had no adequate words, no healing platitudes. Katerina merely stepped closer, slipped one arm around his waist and laid her head on his shoulder. Whether Max realized it or not, she was telling him she cared. She understood.

Her heart sped as logic flew out the window and she admitted one more thing. She was also falling in love with him.

Max didn't know how to react to her empathy. He didn't want to hurt Katerina's feelings, but he also couldn't afford to present a weak image. His job had to come first, at least outwardly. But what he really wanted to do was pull her closer and tilt her chin up so he could kiss her.

He would not act on his urge, of course. That would be totally out of character for an FBI agent on duty. Instead, he stepped away. "I thought you wanted to watch the parade."

"Only if that's what you're going to do."

Nodding, Max agreed. "It makes sense. You

may spot Kyle in the crowd and can point him out to me."

She shivered. "I hope I don't."

"You should be hoping that you do," Max countered. "Without his fingerprints or DNA it's going to be difficult to locate him."

"I know. I have been watching, but mostly because he sounded so determined when he came to the diner. I trust the Lord. I do. I just figure He gave me a brain to use for something besides a place to hang a hat."

"Well put." Max had to chuckle. "You do have a way with words."

"English was going to be my major in college before I decided to become a horse trainer."

Starting off, he paced himself to match Katerina. "What are your plans now?"

She huffed. "You mean besides staying alive? Beats me. I'd like to go back to working at the ranch. Since that's not going to happen, I guess I'll do whatever I have to, to survive. A girl has to eat."

"Maybe you need a pet. Have you thought about getting a watchdog when you move out of the hotel?"

"Another mouth to feed? Not really, although that isn't a bad idea. Not a pup, though. I wouldn't be able to train it while I'm at work." She began to smile wistfully. "I'd ask to adopt that black lab from the ranch if she hadn't recently had a litter. She's sweet and sensible. And not hyper like your Opal."

"I prefer to call it enthusiasm," Max said with a lopsided smile. "I'd give serious consideration to getting a watchdog if I were you."

"Why do I need a dog when I have *you*?" Her eyes twinkled and made him grin until he recalled the parameters of his mission.

"I won't be here much longer," Max warned roughly. "I've already told you that."

"Yeah, I know. I was just teasing. First I have to find a new apartment or talk my former landlord into fixing up the place that was trashed. I actually haven't wanted to think that far ahead."

"Well, you should."

They had traveled the length of Park Street and were approaching Main again. Crowds thickened. Opal stayed close to her partner's left with Katerina on the right. The first few floats had already passed.

"Here comes Dad."

"I see him. And the deputies the sheriff promised as escorts. Everything looks good."

Although he kept scanning the boisterous crowd he was fully aware of the woman beside him. How could he not be? She was making him crazy. Strong and resilient like a warrior and yet soft and gentle as a kitten, she was so close they were almost touching. And *almost* was not enough for him. Not nearly enough. All he'd have to do was lift his arm and it would be around her waist or her shoulders. Katerina had not objected before. He was sure she wouldn't this time, either.

Just as he started to act on the whim she gasped and pointed. "There! Across the street in front of the florist's. See the scruffy-looking guy with the black T-shirt?"

"The one behind the woman with the stroller?"

"Yes! That's Kyle. I know it is."

Max reached for his radio and called in their position. "I'm going to be in foot pursuit. Send somebody to watch Katerina. She's right across Main from the florist shop." He eyed her. "She's going to wait here."

"I am not."

"Yes, you are. I don't want to have to worry about you while I'm taking a prisoner into custody."

"But…"

He gave her his most severe stare. "Do it."

"Yes, sir."

That was good enough for Max. As soon as he spotted the uniform of a deputy coming their way he shouldered through the line of revelers along the curb and jogged across the street. The high school band was marching by and he zigzagged between trumpeters and drummers.

One quick glance ahead told him that his quarry had noticed him and was on the run. So, it was a positive ID. Perfect. The sooner he captured Katerina's stalker and got him to talk, the sooner they could tie up at least a portion of the case. Kyle was the key. Kyle, and the diamonds the Duprees wanted badly enough to kill for.

Katerina stood on tiptoe to watch Max go. One hand shaded her eyes. If she hadn't wanted so desperately to please him she would have broken her coerced promise and followed, although discretely.

If anyone had asked her which marchers had passed since Max's departure she couldn't have said. All she cared about was keeping him in sight. That soon proved impossible. One foot on the base of a lamppost raised her higher and gave her a last glimpse before he passed out of view.

Sighing and resigned to the wait, she let herself down and leaned against the post. An emptiness she had not felt before was impossible to deny. If the sense of loss was this overwhelming just watching him cross the street, what was it going to be like when she had to bid him a final goodbye?

The thought of never seeing Max again settled in her heart and mind to steal any semblance of hope. Of joy. Pride would not let her throw herself at him, particularly when he kept reminding her his presence here in South Fork was temporary. So unless he expressed affection toward her, she was going to have to stand there and hold back her tears as she watched him leave for good.

Did hugs count? she wondered. Nope. Not the kind they had shared so far. He'd simply been comforting her after a crisis. When she'd tried to hug him at the park he'd acted almost embarrassed and had backed away. That was not a good sign. Not good at all. Now, if he had kissed her...

Imagining his kiss made her tremble, made her stomach flutter like butterflies feasting on the bright yellow wild mustard flowers so prevalent on the rolling hills around South Fork.

Someone touched her arm, snapping her from her reverie. She looked around, expecting to see the deputy who was coming to watch over her. A hard metal object poked her in the ribs at the same instant.

"Don't make a sound," Kyle warned, sneering. "You and I are going for a little walk. If you make a fuss and I start shooting, who knows how many kids might get hurt."

She couldn't move, couldn't take a step, until he gave her arm a jerk. Where was Max? Where was the deputy who was supposed to be there with her?

Katerina found her balance and her voice. "All right. Stay calm. I'll go with you."

"Knew you were a smart girl." He signaled with a toss of his head. "This way."

Eyes wide, she desperately cast around for any kind of help that wouldn't cause her abductor to panic and pull the trigger. There was no one except innocent, clueless civilians, so she didn't dare call out or try to escape his painful grasp.

An incoherent prayer for deliverance formed in her mind. No rescuer appeared. She staggered, tripped, tried to think far enough beyond the moment to know what to do.

One thing was certain.

Survival was totally up to her.

FOURTEEN

Max had rendezvoused with several deputies when they got another call. Earpiece receivers kept him from eavesdropping but the grave looks on their faces told him plenty.

"You're sure?" one of them replied before turning to Max to report, "Reynolds is on scene. There's no sign of the Garwood woman where you said she'd be."

"Tell him to look again. She's wearing a pink shirt."

"Sorry, Agent West."

Every nerve in his body was firing. "All right. You men keep searching for the runner in the black T-shirt. I lost him in that alley over there. I'm going back for Katerina. She can't have strayed far."

Time was his enemy, Max concluded as he wheeled and took off with Opal at his side. Had it been long enough since he'd lost sight of Kyle for the man to have doubled back? He doubted it, but this wasn't his town so maybe there was a shortcut.

"Opal, heel." He shouted over the noise of the celebrants, assuming a runner's pace. If only she were a tracking dog like Harper's German shepherd he'd be able to send her to find Katerina. Some K-9s were cross-trained if they showed aptitude but he hadn't seen the need for adding to his dog's repertoire until now.

The partners crossed Main at the corner by Park. Anxiety had sapped some of the stamina he needed to continue. Max paused in the spot where he'd last seen Katerina and scanned the crowd, looking for the right color hair and her neon pink T-shirt. It was like searching for the proverbial needle in a haystack, only he was looking for one special lady in a sea of moving, shifting bodies, many of whom were tall enough to hide her.

"Katerina!"

He turned the opposite direction, cupped a hand around his mouth and shouted again. "Katerina! Where are you?"

Opal had been straining at her leash since they'd reached the familiar corner. Now, she yipped.

Max checked her body language and started to ignore her until he saw the rapid wag of her tail. Dressed to work, she was not usually that amiable. "Katerina?" he repeated.

The eager dog pulled harder, actually scratching at the pavement with her front paws. He took one last look around, then heeded to his canine partner.

"All right, Opal. That's as good a direction to go as any." He keyed his mic. "This is West. I'm headed south on Park. No sign of the Garwood woman yet but my dog is pulling me this way so I'm going to take a chance."

"Copy," someone radioed back. "We're converging on your location. Deputy Reynolds has already found a couple of folks who think they saw Katerina leaving."

"Was she alone?" Max's throat tightened.

"Nobody was sure. Proceed with caution."

As if they had to tell him! Caution was ingrained in any bomb-detecting specialist. Except that he had already broken protocol by racing around as if he and Opal were two ants crossing hot pavement.

All the time his feet and brain were racing he was searching the distance, praying he'd get a glimpse of Katerina.

Over there? Max's hope jumped, then crashed. It wasn't her. *There?* No. Same color clothing but wrong wearer. He had to force himself to inhale and exhale instead of holding his breath every time he thought he saw her.

Opal's nose was to the ground now. Max knew she'd never had actual practice as a tracking dog but apparently her instinct to find her new friend was strong enough to carry her, at least this far.

Rather than give any commands and possibly confuse the dog, he let her run as fast as she could go with him on the other end of her leash. Clearly, she could have outdistanced him without effort but Max had to hold on or he might lose her, too.

His legs ached and there was a painful stitch in his side. Nevertheless he pressed on. They crossed the main picnic area, then skirted the restrooms. Beyond lay an overflow parking lot where many of the floats and other participants had gathered after the parade.

Opal suddenly pulled to the side, nearly tripping Max. He spun to follow. And saw Bertrand Garwood's classic Packard.

No, no! Not that. Max's heart fell. Opal was headed straight for the same car she'd alerted on before. If she was after that odd odor instead of following Katerina's trail, he'd wasted precious time.

The ranch foreman was no longer behind the wheel but the mayor was once again polishing chrome. "Did you see her?" Max shouted. "Have you seen Katerina?"

Garwood paused and scowled. "No. Why?"

"I think she's been kidnapped."

"Don't be ridiculous. There's no real crime in

this town." His wrinkled deepened. "At least there wasn't until her boyfriend showed up."

Max was in no mood to argue. Expecting Opal to stop to sniff the car's trunk, he was astonished to see her put her nose to the ground again and take off.

"Wait a minute," he called to Garwood. "She went past here. Are you sure you didn't see her?"

"I told you I didn't."

"Where's your foreman? McCabe."

"Filling his gut, I imagine. Check the food tables."

Holding a straining Opal in check, Max radioed his position to the deputies and suggested exactly that. If one of them could locate McCabe, he might be able to tell them more.

"I'm going to follow my K-9 until she finds Katerina or loses the trail," Max said, knowing Garwood was eavesdropping and a little surprised at his interest.

The older man stood back, reached into his pocket and fisted a keychain. "You can borrow my car if you promise to take good care of it."

Well, well. "Thanks, but I need to be on the ground with the dog," Max told him. "If you decide to cruise around and look for her, give us plenty of space. I don't want anything to disturb the scent trail."

He didn't glance back to see what Katerina's

father was doing after that. All he cared about was giving Opal the best chance to succeed. When all this was over and they were back in Billings, he was going to suggest she be trained in tracking people as well as detecting explosives. That would work as long as he was able to tell her exactly which job he wanted her to do at any given time.

Right now, all he wanted was Katerina. The nagging notion of losing her, for whatever reason, ate at him until his physical pain and fatigue became secondary.

A shuddering breath filled his lungs. This could not be happening. He'd vowed to look after her and had failed. It didn't matter that he'd thought a deputy was taking over for him. He should have waited with her until the other guard arrived.

Opal barked once. Max faltered, tripped and almost fell. With a mighty lunge the dog ripped the end of the long lead from his hand and began to run like a greyhound chasing a rabbit.

"Opal! Stop! Heel!"

Those commands made her seem to go even faster. Max was both livid and distressed. In all the years they had been working partners, Opal had never failed to come when called. Never. If he lost her it would be his fault. Just as it was his fault he'd lost Katerina.

Instead of slowing him down, the weight of his emotional burdens gave Max his second wind.

Without a dog to handle he was free to run at his top speed, arms pumping, knees lifting higher as he pounded through the park.

Drying ground and dead grass made it harder to pick out Opal's coat coloring in the distance but her dark vest stood out. So did the bright white FBI printed on the side. Max saw her slow, circle, then take off again. This time she was giving voice like a hunting hound who was about to tree its prey.

Max interpreted the signs and pressed on until he thought his legs would buckle. Adrenaline fueled his mad dash.

Thoughts of Katerina kept him going.

There was no doubt in Katerina's mind that Kyle would shoot her if she tried to flee. Fear kept her from thinking logically until he had forced her through the park and tried to push her into his waiting car at the far edge of an overflow parking lot. That snapped her out of it enough to try to reason with him.

"Look, don't you suppose that if I knew where Vern had hidden the diamonds I'd have already gotten them?"

"Maybe you did."

She could tell he was confused. Good. Anything that gave her an edge was a plus. "If I had, do you think I'd still be slinging hash at a diner?"

"You might, if you were smart."

"If I was really smart, I'd have figured out that Vern was a crook long before he got me into so much trouble."

"Yeah, well." The wiry man gestured with the pistol. "Get in. We're goin' for a ride and you're gonna show me where those rocks are, or else."

"Are you listening to me?" Anger began to bolster her courage and she raised her voice. "I have nothing left. No home, barely any personal belongings, nothing. I do not know anything about any diamonds and I never did. Vern wouldn't have trusted me with that information because he knew I was too honest. That was why I was such a good cover for him. People trusted me. And with good reason."

"Well, we don't trust you."

Katerina's eyebrows arched. "*We?* Who's we? I thought you were the one who's been stalking me."

"I was. I am." Looking agitated, he raked his fingers through his rumpled, oily hair. "Are you gonna get in this car or do I have to shoot you?"

"You can't be that dumb."

"Hey, show some respect," Kyle snapped.

"Look," she said, speaking slowly and choosing her words with care, "if you shoot me and I *do* happen to know where Vern hid anything, you're up the creek without a paddle. Who else can you ask? Who else was close enough to him to know his secrets?"

"Okay, we'll split it. If you're as broke as you say, you can use some cash."

Katerina sighed. If she agreed to a split to stall for time until someone could rescue her, she'd be digging her own grave because Kyle would then be sure she knew too much. If she refused, he might soon decide she was useless. Either way, she lost.

Father, I could use some help here, she prayed. *I've always tried to do the right thing, to be a good Christian, but I can't see any way out of this.*

One thing was certain. She was not getting into that car. No, sirree.

A blur of color entered the edge of her vision. It was moving so fast it was airborne before she could react. Fortunately, the same was true of her kidnapper.

Opal hit him so hard in the chest he fell backward and thumped his head on the ground. The gun went flying. Stunned, Katerina stood there gaping. The dog was growling and drooling on Kyle's face. His eyeballs looked as though they were about to pop out of their sockets, and he was thrashing and pushing at her to escape.

Katerina frantically looked for Max. He wasn't in sight. Therefore, she had two choices. She could either try to grab the gun, back Opal and hope

Max arrived very soon, or she could run away to save herself, hoping the valiant dog would follow. Given her recent belief that her life was about to end abruptly, she opted for flight.

"Opal, come!" she screeched, rounding the parked car and heading into a grove of live oaks for cover. She didn't dare look back.

Her last call was, "Opal-l-l-l!

She heard a single gunshot. Her heart sank. Grasping the broad, rough trunk of one of the ancient trees, she peeked around just in time to see Kyle's car speed off.

"No, no, no. Not Opal." Katerina was bereft.

She slid to the ground beneath the tree and began to weep. In seconds, a warm, rough tongue was drying her cheeks. "Opal! Oh, baby!"

A quick once-over showed no injuries. Katerina's tears turned to those of pure joy. She hugged the brown-and-white K-9 close, buried her face against its shoulder, and began to sob away all the tension and fear. "Thank you, Jesus."

Max saw the whole thing. Opal downed Katerina's kidnapper but the guy was far from out of the fight. The dog held him as best she could without biting the way an apprehension specialist would. Katerina bolted. The perp wiggled loose. Reached his gun. Raised it.

After that, details blurred and overlapped.

Opal and Katerina were both running. The man aimed and fired. Katerina ducked behind a tree but whether she was hit or not was unknown. The same went for Opal. She looked as if she'd stumbled or made a dive for cover. Or been shot.

Max drew his own gun on the run. "Federal agent. Drop your weapon."

Instead, the perp burned rubber in his escape.

"Katerina!" It was more of a gasp than a shout and all Max could manage for the moment.

No one answered. His heart was already at the breaking point. He fought to stay on his feet. Imagination was his worst enemy. In his mind he visualized another terrible loss. Another failure. This couldn't have happened, yet it had.

Lungs ready to burst, head pounding, he once again bellowed, "Katerina! Opal!" in a voice that was breaking despite his efforts to sound forceful and in command.

"Max? Over here!"

His head snapped around. He could manage a few more steps even if they used his last shred of strength.

And then he saw her. She was hurrying toward him, apparently unhurt, and Opal was at her side.

Max used every ounce of self-control to try to keep his reactions in check. He failed. In seconds, he had engulfed Katerina in a smothering embrace. His tears dampened her silky hair. The shuddering of her whole body told him that she, too, was weeping.

And so he held her like that, thanking the God he had once turned his back on and feeling so much abject relief he could hardly process the sensations.

There was joy, of course, but so much more. Peace. Assuredness. Rightness. And above all, a sense of loving and being loved that Max had never dreamed could be so strong. So absolute. So perfect.

Even as deputies began to surround them and ask about the gunshot that had brought them running, Max held tightly to Katerina and felt faithful Opal leaning against his legs, acting possessive and sharing the precious moment.

If he'd had his way, he and Katerina would never have parted.

FIFTEEN

Debriefing seemed to take forever. Katerina couldn't help yawning. She and Max were seated side by side on a weathered wooden bench at the edge of the picnic area while the sheriff interrogated her.

"I told you. I don't know who Kyle is other than he used to be a friend of Vern Kowalski's," she said, sighing wearily because she was sick and tired of answering the same questions over and over. "I don't know his last name, where he lives or who he hangs out with. I only met him one time before he came to the diner and threatened me. If he hadn't reminded me who he was then, I wouldn't have remembered him at all."

"I think we're done here," Max stated. "I'm going to take Ms. Garwood back to her hotel. If you have further questions you can phone me and I'll contact her."

Tate scowled. "Just a second here, Agent West, this is my jurisdiction."

Max stood, pulling Katerina up with him as he took her arm. "Agreed. But this witness is mine. I'm putting her into protective custody."

She could tell the deputies were waiting to see which authority would prevail. No doubt it would be her special agent. Truth to tell, she didn't care who won as long as she got to take a shower and change clothes to rid herself of any traces of Kyle's disgusting touch.

The sheriff backed off. "Okay. Take her to the hotel. I've already put out a BOLO for the car you described. If and when we find it I may need you for a positive ID."

"Our pleasure," Max said brusquely.

Katerina leaned his way ever so slightly. *Our*, he had said. *Our pleasure, as in "the two of us."* Her heart warmed and she might have commented if she had not been too bone-weary to think straight.

As Max led her away, he asked, "Are you okay?"

The urge to tease him about such a ridiculous question popped into her head. She squelched it immediately. He wasn't asking only what his words expressed. He was asking much more. How should she answer? How much truth was he ready to hear?

Playing it safe for the present, she merely nodded and murmured, "I'm fine," then counteracted her assurance by stumbling.

Max caught her in his arms, righted her, then took her hand. "When was the last time you ate?"

"Um, breakfast?"

"That's what I thought." He began to steer her toward the tables of food. "You need a hamburger."

"I need a nap."

"First a burger."

Katerina sighed audibly. "I can't believe you're thinking about food at a time like this." When she glanced up at him he had arched one eyebrow.

"A time like what?" Max asked.

"This." Spreading her arms she included the scene before them. "Most of them may be clueless but you know I just got shot at. My stomach is twisted into knots and I'm so exhausted I can hardly keep putting one foot in front of the other. I am *not* hungry."

"You still need to try to eat," he insisted. "The mistake a lot of people make is letting their stress get in the way of common sense. If you allow your body to suffer because your mind is taxed, you're playing right into the hands of your enemies."

Katerina shook her head and met his steady gaze. "I wish you'd quit making such good sense. All I want to do is crawl into a cave somewhere and hibernate like a bear until this is all over."

"Soon." Max was grinning at an elderly gentleman in a Hawaiian print shirt. He was flipping burgers on a grill. Arrayed on a long table beside him was everything to go with the meat. "Is it all right with you if we grab a couple of burgers to go?"

"Fine by me. Better take beans, too, though. My wife made 'em and she's real proud."

Following his line of sight, Katerina saw a familiar woman dishing up baked beans. "Let's just go. I'll eat something later."

"What's the matter?"

"I want to leave, that's all." To her chagrin he was studying her and obviously seeing more truth than she was comfortable with.

Instead of acquiescing, Max grinned widely and handed her a plate, then moved on. What else could Katerina do? She certainly didn't want to attract more attention than she already had. Head down, she used tongs to put a hamburger patty and bun on her paper plate and stayed close to her protector.

The older woman met Max's smile with one of her own, taking in his uniform and Opal's vest. "We're so glad to see the FBI helping out in South Fork," she said. "About time, considering. Beans?"

Katerina looked up. Saw the woman's countenance change, her smile vanish.

"Yes, thanks," Max said, presenting his plate.

"And I'm glad to have the help of a trustworthy citizen like Ms. Garwood. She's been a tremendous help to our investigation. I don't know what we'd do without her."

Katerina was not too worn-out to see the humor in the woman's reactions. Her jaw sagged, along with the spoonful of baked beans she'd been about to serve. The only reason it landed on a plate was because Max moved his in time to catch the spill.

"Mercy," the woman said when she finally found her voice, "I had no idea."

Max wasn't done. His admiring gaze rested on Katerina and made her blush more when he said, "Absolutely. As a matter of fact, when all this is over, I plan to recommend her for a citizen's commendation."

"On second thought, I believe I will have some beans," Katerina said with a demure smile. "Thank you."

As they made their way to a nearby table to eat, she couldn't help enjoying the sense of triumph. "How did you know she was one of my worst critics?"

"I'm a profiler, remember?"

Katerina huffed. "You'd hardly need professional training to tell how she felt. Did you see the dirty look she gave me?"

"Yes, and I took advantage of the opportunity to praise you. I hope you don't mind."

"Only if you truly meant those nice things you said. I have been trying to help. There just isn't much I can do and it's terribly frustrating."

"I know. You get high points for trying." He stepped away from the table for a moment to pick up two bottles of water and handed one to her.

"Thanks." As soon as she had slaked her thirst, Katerina took a few bites of her hamburger, then asked, "Is there really a special commendation for helpful citizens?"

When he almost choked on his food she knew the answer. As soon as he stopped coughing, he said, "Not exactly."

Her laugh was easy and joyful. "You are so bad, Special Agent West. Aren't you ashamed of yourself?"

"Not much." Max laid his hand over hers and smiled with evident fondness. "Anything I can do to make your life better after I'm gone is worth it."

The mention of his leaving dampened Katerina's good mood the way a heavy rainstorm would have wiped out the picnic atmosphere. Although she didn't pull her hand away she did tense. He was like a loop of tape, always coming back to the fact he was only a temporary fixture in her life. She knew that. She did. It was painful enough without constant reminders.

And, considering what she had just gone through—and survived—she figured she had nothing to lose if she said, "I wish you didn't have to go. I'm really going to miss... Opal."

At the mention of her name, the panting dog peeked out from her cooler spot under the table. She was drooling.

Max released Katerina's hand and abruptly got to his feet. "You two wait here. I'm going to go see if they have an extra burger or two that I can feed to my partner."

Laying a hand on the boxer's broad, smooth head, Katerina made a sound of disgust that caught the dog's attention, so she talked directly to her. "Yes, girl, that was a romantic overture I was trying to make. He sure ducked it fast, didn't he?"

The happy dog panted more. "You look like you're smiling. Are you? Have you heard other women throw themselves at your partner? I imagine you have. He's a real hunk, isn't he? Mature and sensible but not stuffy. Don't tell him I said so, but he's just about perfect."

A voice behind her asked, "What's perfect?" Max had returned.

"Your K-9," Katerina said, feeling her cheeks flame.

"Can't argue with that," Max said. He resumed his seat on the bench and was starting to break off pieces of a plain burger patty for Opal when he suddenly stopped moving and canted his head slightly.

Katerina had seen him receive radio messages

often enough to know he was listening through the earpiece. Her eyes never left his face until she heard him say, "Copy," and start to get up.

"Bring your plate and let's go," Max said. "I'll feed Opal the rest after we're in the car."

"Why? What happened?" The gravity of his expression gave her the shivers. So did the stiffness of his movements and the way he kept scanning the crowd, not that he had ever stopped. But he had been acting a bit less paranoid for the past half hour or so.

"They think they located the car that tried to take you. We'll swing by their location on our way to the hotel and you can make a positive identification."

"I hope I can," Katerina said. She had to take two steps for every one of his and ended up almost jogging. Max had been right. Eating had helped her recover her stamina.

"Think. Did you touch the vehicle at all? Anywhere? Maybe when he tried to shove you in?"

"I—I might have. It all happened so fast I'm not positive. I do know I resisted."

"That may be enough," Max said. "When we get there we'll see if you left any fingerprints on the side where he stopped with you. After they have the car towed to the police garage they can have techs go over it more thoroughly, but if we can make an ID sooner, all the better."

"What about Kyle? Did they catch him?"

Max was stoic. He was also on full guard. "No. Just the car. And the engine was fairly cool. In this heat it's impossible to tell how long it may have been parked."

"Meaning, he could have doubled back to town again?"

It didn't give her a shred of comfort when Max nodded and said, "That's exactly what the sheriff thinks. They scoured the woods and didn't find any sign of him."

Katerina and Max joined the only deputy left to guard the car. It had been abandoned near the entrance to Yosemite Park. Max had to admit the high country was beautiful. If it had not been hiding a stalker and erstwhile kidnapper, he figured he would have appreciated the gorgeous scenery a lot more.

Beside him in the SUV, Katerina gasped and pointed. "There. That's it."

"Looks right to me. Anything special grab you?"

"Yes. Now that I see it, I remember a half-peeled window decal. It's a picture of Half Dome. I think it was in the corner of the left rear window." She leaned forward to peer through the windshield. "There! See?"

"Yes," Max said. "But we're going to need more

proof than that. I imagine those decals are common around here."

"I don't think so. Mostly tourists buy them."

"A good point." He brought his black vehicle to a stop behind the patrol car, got out and introduced himself. "Special Agent Max West," he said, offering his hand and checking out the man's badge and name tag as he approached. "You may be the only local law officer I haven't already met, Deputy Cox."

"I've been working the highways," the deputy said. "Might not have noticed this if the guy had left it inside the park. This time of year is so busy up here it's ridiculous. Come the Fourth of July the traffic will be backed up for miles."

"No sign of the driver?"

"Nope. Just the car."

"Okay," Max said. "Have you checked for prints or trace evidence yet?"

"Sheriff Tate said to wait for you."

Max could tell the young man was probably a rookie. He sure was nervous enough to be. "Okay. No problem. I'll see if I can find a few prints on the outside before you have it towed."

"Yes, sir."

"Keep a sharp eye on my SUV and passenger, will you? I'd hate to lose either."

"You got a police dog in there, too?"

"Yes." Max nodded as he went to work. He'd told Katerina to stay in his car but there was no telling what she might actually do. She was the best and worst kind of woman. She didn't take orders well at all, yet was intelligent and savvy enough to figure things out on her own, so she wasn't as helpless as she looked. Her guileless blue eyes and fair skin beneath a wreath of golden hair gave her an air of innocence that was totally false. Not only was she brave, she was also so smart she sometimes scared him.

And that wasn't the only thing that had him on edge. He scanned the nearby forest, watching for movement. Open, hilly fields colored yellow by dry grass were bad enough. Spotting a predator lurking amid stands of Ponderosa pines and live oaks was next to impossible.

If a perp fired on them they'd never see it coming, Max concluded. The hair at the nape of his neck prickled at the thought. He listened to his gut and tensed, prepared to duck.

The instant he started to turn he heard the crack and whine of a high-caliber rifle cartridge slicing the air.

Max hollered, "Get down!"

His heart nearly pounded out of his chest when Katerina let out an ear-piercing scream.

SIXTEEN

Katerina saw Max fall.

He dropped as though his legs had been knocked out from under him.

Opal set up a terrible racket, her barks and growls echoing inside the closed SUV as she screamed.

Whether it was because of Max's shouted order or by sheer instinct, she flatted herself to the seat as best she could considering all the specialized electronic equipment that was in the way.

Long seconds passed. She could feel her pulse thrumming in her temples, coursing through her veins. Was it over? Was it safe to look, to see if Max was wounded?

She knew better than to show herself too soon. She also knew that the man she loved might be injured. Might need her. At this point she didn't care whether the special agent returned her affection or not. His life might be ebbing away while she lay there, too petrified to act.

That was not going to happen, Katerina vowed. She wasn't foolish enough to simply sit up and present another target, but she could still slip out of the SUV on the opposite side and crawl around it until she got a better look at the scene.

Opal was still carrying on as if they were under attack so she chose to leave the dog behind for its own safety.

The first thing Katerina did was drop to all fours, look beneath the high vehicle and locate Max. He was moving fluidly. And his gun was drawn. He was okay!

"Thank you, God," she whispered, meaning the simple prayer with all her heart.

What about the young deputy? All she could see were his feet and legs sticking out from behind the open door of his car. He was closer than Max so she made a dash for him. And saw that he was gritting his teeth and grasping his bloody arm!

"How can I help you?" Katerina asked, realizing that adrenaline had boosted the strength of her voice as soon as Max shouted back at her.

"Nothing. Stay put," he yelled.

"The deputy's hit!" she answered. "What should I do?"

Max's reply was the human equivalent of Opal's growling. Katerina didn't care. She'd doctored enough animals to know that her first move should be to stop or slow the bleeding with pressure, not a tourniquet. There were no rags handy but she did spot a handful of napkins on the seat, apparently left over from the deputy's lunch. That would be a start.

Stripping off his tie, too, she struggled to get him to listen to her. "Let go and let me pad it," she said. "See? Napkins. We have to stop the bleeding."

Although he nodded and seemed to understand, his hand was clamped so tightly to his injury she couldn't pry it loose. "Let go. Let me help you," she shouted, as if volume might get through his instinct to keep his hand firmly in place.

When a strong arm reached past her and jerked the deputy's hand loose she almost screamed again. Of course it was Max. Who else would have risked his own life to reach the patrol car?

Working together as if trained as a team, Katerina and Max placed the wad of napkins, then wrapped the tie around the man's arm to keep them in place before allowing him to resume his hold.

"I've called for backup and an ambulance," Max told the injured man. "Understand? Help is on the way."

Katerina had expected a little praise, if not another faux award for bravery. Instead, she got Max's most disapproving stare. "What did you think you were doing? Huh? You could have been shot, too."

"But I wasn't."

"Not this time. I'm sure I was the target but considering the shooter's lousy aim he could just as easily have hit you." His scowl was so deep his eyebrows almost met in the middle of his forehead. "Keep your head down. The day isn't over yet."

"Not funny," she countered.

"It wasn't meant to be." Grasping her shoulders he glared so hard she wanted to look away. She couldn't. There was more than one emotion coloring his expression. Anger was obvious, of course, but there was also so much angst it mesmerized her. Not only that, he was right. She had acted rashly. Yes, she'd had good reason to, but that didn't excuse folly.

Meeting his stern gaze, she nodded. "I'm sorry. You're right. I shouldn't have left the car."

"Well, that's *something*. Did you see him go down?"

Katerina felt that the whole, unvarnished truth was the best course so she held nothing back. "No. When I heard the shot it was you I was watching." Unshed tears pooled. "I—I thought you'd been hit and needed help. That's why I got out. But when I saw you moving and you looked okay, I noticed that the deputy wasn't." She sniffled. "I'm not as good a person as you think I am. I only risked my life because of you."

The agent's expression became unreadable.

He released her shoulders and sat back on his haunches. His jaw worked. No words came out. Given his earlier chastisement, Katerina was relieved. And penitent.

"I really am sorry. It was just something I had to do. You should understand. After all, that's how you function."

"No," Max said soberly. "I'm certified to do this job. You're a horse trainer, not an FBI agent or a cop. It's high time you got that through your head."

Katerina was more than willing to let him rant if that was what he chose to do. She deserved a good chewing out. And Max's motives were clear. What he said and did was for her benefit, unlike Bertrand, whose main focus was on himself and his so-called reputation.

"I was wrong," Katerina said, trying again to make peace. "Very wrong. I was thinking about my own feelings instead of assessing the danger. It was stupid. I should have stayed put."

"Yes, you should have." He eyed the injured man. "It's beside the point that you may have saved a life by following the urge to check on this officer."

Sirens in the background grew louder. Backup and medical assistance was near.

The relaxing set of Max's jaw and a softening of his glance gave her hope of forgiveness and the approach of paramedics lifted her spirits. That also loosened her tongue enough to ask, "So do I finally qualify for the good citizen's award you mentioned?"

He rolled his eyes and cautiously peered over the side of the patrol car, watching reinforcements arrive. "You qualify for something, all right. I'm just not sure what to call it. Not in polite company."

Before Katerina could come up with a suitable retort he'd gotten to his feet and holstered his sidearm.

"Is it safe?"

"For me, not for you. Stay down until we've made sure the shooter is long gone."

"He probably is, right? I mean, with all the police cars he must have taken off."

"Assumptions like that can get you killed," Max warned. "Just like the idea that if you're on a rescue mission you can't be shot." His icy stare returned. "You can either stay put right there or I'll have the sheriff's men cuff you and throw you in the back of one of their cars."

"You wouldn't dare!"

She knew otherwise when Max gave her a lopsided smile and said, "Try me."

"I wish I had the whole team here with me," Max told Dylan O'Leary when he finally checked in with headquarters again. "Have you had any success tracking down the owner of the prints I took from the car at the park?"

"Yeah. I think so. I'm sending a mug shot to your computer and cell. There was a petty criminal associated with Kowalski years ago. It was a juvenile offense so the records were sealed until I opened them."

"I do not need details you're not supposed to know," Max told him. "Just give me a last name."

"Take your pick. I found three besides Smith and Jones. He went by Kinder, Farth and Wilson."

"Sounds like a law firm."

The tech chuckled. "That was my first thought. Then I got to thinking he may have added another alias since then. I would have."

"Yes, but you have a devious mind," Max joked. "I don't think this guy is too bright."

"Doesn't have to be bright to be lethal."

"No kidding. He shot a deputy yesterday. At least I think it was him. Makes me wonder why the shooter didn't try for me."

"Maybe he did."

"I thought of that. Trajectory of the bullet makes it a remote possibility."

"What about the girl? Katerina Garwood? Have you gotten any more out of her after this last scare?"

Max sobered. "I already told you. She's given

us everything she knows. What we can't figure out is where Kowalski stashed those missing diamonds."

"Or where he got the money to buy them in the first place? It's my guess he stole from Dupree and decided it was easier to hide his sudden wealth as little stones than to lug around a suitcase full of cash."

"I agree. What about a getaway plan? Have you turned up any solid leads?"

"No. If Kowalski intended to skip town before he was arrested, he wasn't going to fly. At least not under his own name. There's no record of ticket purchases." Dylan paused. "Not even a single seat."

"To show he was going alone? I get it. I wish you had found some record. It would uphold Katerina's innocence."

"Hey, you trust her."

"I do. Implicitly. But that doesn't mean the rest of the people in her life feel the same. You wouldn't believe her father's rotten attitude."

"Is that your problem, buddy? Are you thinking of stepping in as an older brother?"

"No way! Besides, I do not think of her as a little sister. She's every bit a grown woman. Boy, is she."

"Uh-oh. Here we go again. Another one bites the dust."

"Don't be ridiculous. She lives here and I do not intend to get involved in a long-distance romance."

Dylan laughed into the phone. "Sounds to me like you already are. Talk to you later."

"Yeah. Later."

Picturing Katerina kneeling beside the bleeding deputy and trying to doctor him, Max had a moment when he yearned to take her in his arms again and hold her tight. She was more than pretty. She was extraordinary. And the more he saw of her, the more his admiration blossomed.

That's all it is, Max insisted. Countering that thought made him clench his jaw. He might be able to fool his team and the general population but he wasn't fooling himself. He loved Katerina Garwood even more than he loved his K-9 partner. And that was a lot.

Katerina didn't spot another note shoved under the door of her hotel room until she'd finished dressing the following morning. Recognizing the paper, she immediately phoned Max.

"West."

"A note. Another note." She was nearly hysterical. "You have to come to my room."

"On my way."

She managed to unlock the door in the seconds before he got there and stood back. The instant he threw open the door she raised both hands. "Stop! Don't step on it."

Max skidded to a halt.

"I didn't touch it," she said, trembling. "How did he get this close?" Her eyes darted to the narrow hallway. "He had to be right here!"

"Not if he paid somebody else to deliver it."

"If that's supposed to be comforting, it isn't."

She stepped back, leaving the door open as the agent used a glove to handle the paper. He took it to the dresser to unfold and read.

Katerina peered past his broad shoulder. Her vision began to blur. It was worse than she'd expected. Not only did it threaten her, it clearly promised death to Bertrand Garwood—and her dear horse Moonlight—if she failed to show up at the ranch at an appointed time and disclose information on the location of the diamond stash.

"What—what can I do?" she asked.

Max was already on the phone to the sheriff's office. Judging by his half of the conversation they were formulating a plan.

"That's right," Max said. "Garwood. I need you to get in touch with him and convince him to leave his ranch for the time being. And tell him to put a guard on his property, particularly the horses."

When Katerina saw Max scowl she assumed he was being told that her father had already refused to comply. That figured. If he was anything, he was stubborn. And proud, which was why he had disowned her in the first place.

"All right. We can filter in on foot, a few at a time. I'll meet you in the lobby of my hotel at eleven and we'll go over strategy. Just make sure everybody stays well hidden. This guy has already wounded one deputy and I know he won't hesitate to shoot another."

"No." Katerina grabbed Max's arm, but he ignored her protest. The note had insisted she come alone. If they broke that rule and arrived like a posse, surely her dad and Moonlight would be killed in retaliation.

"Yes," Max said, looking as if he meant his terse comment for her. He bid the sheriff goodbye and turned to give Katerina his full attention.

She raised her hands, palms out. "We can't do it your way. The note said no police." As she realized the full extent of the command her eyes widened. "That means you, too."

"Oh, no. I'm not letting you go anywhere without me so don't even think of trying it. Understand?" He was scowling.

"Yes, but…"

"No buts. I'll let you phone the ranch and try to convince your dad to leave but you are *not* going out there."

"I have to." Panicky, she pointed to the top of the dresser where the threatening note lay. "They still think I know where Vern hid the diamonds. It's them I need to convince, not my father."

Quietly, calmly, Max cupped her shoulders. "Only if we can be absolutely positive he didn't have anything to do with the illegal operations taking place out of his ranch."

Katerina jerked free. "Of course he didn't! Look at how he's been treating me since you raided the place."

"That might be a good way to cover up his guilt."

She whirled. Paced, then turned. "No way. Not him. He may be a pompous…never mind…but he isn't crooked. I'd stake my life on it."

"I believe you, Katerina. Which is why I've decided you're not going with us when we gather at the ranch again. It's too dangerous. You have nothing to add except to put yourself in unnecessary danger. We'll close in after Kyle gets on scene and grab him. There will be no need for you to leave this room."

Gaping at him, she stared. "You must be joking."

"I have never been more serious."

She fisted her hands on her hips and glared at him. "Give me one good reason why I should take orders from you."

Hesitation on his part took her aback. What did he know about the planned attack that he wasn't revealing? Was it really going to be as dangerous as he'd indicated to the sheriff or was he merely trying to control her? Yes, she loved his powerful persona and forthright way of doing things, but it galled when it was directed at her.

"You can't go. That's all there is to it."

"Not for me, it isn't all. Either you share your reasoning or I'm going, whether you like it or not."

Max came closer. His expression was grim, his gaze steady and uncompromising. When he reached for her again she almost fled. Almost, but not quite.

The touch of his hands on her shoulders was gentle but firm. "It's time for you to put your trust in me the way you want me to trust you."

"I have. I do. I just want…"

In a low, rumbling voice he asked, "What? What do you want, Katerina?"

The intimacy of the moment was so powerful, despite the open door, it wiped her mind of answers the way rain washed summer's dust from the petals of a flower.

Max urged her closer with the slightest pressure.

She slipped her arms around his waist and waited. It was up to him this time. He'd rejected her in the park and she wasn't going to set herself up for another failure.

He lifted her chin with his forefinger and her

heart raced as anticipation flooded through her. His lips brushed hers so gently she wondered if her imagination was playing tricks.

Then he whispered her name with such tenderness she melted into his embrace.

At that moment she would gladly have promised him the moon and then tried to deliver it.

Their kiss deepened. Lingered. Left Max trembling almost as much as Katerina was. The thrill of finally knowing he cared for her was so encompassing she willingly lost herself in it.

Before she could fully regain her senses, Max broke contact, stepped to the door and said, "*That's* why you have to stay here."

Alone, she leaned against the dresser for support. He'd as much as said he loved her. And that kiss... Oh, my. No wonder she had been so unsure about marrying Vern. There was no comparison between the two men. Max was the one. Now all she had to do was...what? Follow his orders?

Breathing deeply and pulling herself together, Katerina realized that letting him walk into danger on her behalf was the *last* thing she'd do. When he had taken her in his arms and kissed her that way he had given her undeniable reasons to stand by his side. Katerina folded her arms and hugged herself, smiling as she recalled every moment of that captivating embrace. Max might be a hotshot government profiler but he didn't have a clue what a woman in love might do. A woman like her.

She glanced at the digital clock on the bedside table. She had hours to come up with her own perfect plan and put it in motion. Or talk herself out of doing something so stupid she'd be forever sorry.

Given her heightened emotions and the way she was unable to force herself to consider staying back while Max risked his life, she figured she was bound to choose with her heart rather than her head. That was okay up to a point. The point where she put herself in real danger.

Ideally, she could reach the ranch early and remove both her mare and her father from the premises before any harm came to them. Or to her.

And then Max would be free to arrest Kyle without incident.

SEVENTEEN

Katerina's mare, Moonlight, was both the easiest potential victim for her to reach and also the most tractable, so she began her rescue efforts there.

Since Kyle expected her to show up to meet him anyway she didn't try to hide the green muscle car the FBI had rented for her. Instead, she parked it in roughly the same place she'd left her ruined truck, one building over. Arriving very early for their appointment did impart a positive feeling but it wasn't nearly as reassuring as being with Max had been.

There were no grooms bustling around, she noticed. That was a little strange but she chalked it up to hot weather and the aftermath of the daylong celebration and parade. Anyone who had partied much at the park or elsewhere was liable to be sleeping it off, and that included the ranch foreman.

Heath McCabe usually managed the Garwood barns pretty well even if he was under the weather.

She couldn't remember one instance when he hadn't at least shown up to make sure that the valuable animals were fed and watered adequately no matter what.

Keeping her eye out for Heath so she could warn him to steer clear for a while, just in case, she checked the chart in the tack room listing Moonlight's new stall and headed straight for it. Each step seemed more perilous. This idea had seemed sound back at the hotel. Now, as the minutes ticked by, the doubts started to creep in.

Reaching the stall, Katerina gazed fondly at Moonlight and took several deep, calming breaths. Her beloved, dapple gray mare had darker ears, nose and long black eyelashes, making her even more striking than she would have been in solid gray. Her beautiful coat had always reminded Katerina of moonlight on snow, although there was precious little of that where they lived. The agile mare's Arabian roots showed in her fine bone and facial features, as did the cross with a Standardbred for greater size.

Although Katerina wasn't the only trainer and rider who could handle her she was definitely the person the horse preferred. That affinity came in handy at times like these. Times when she needed to put a halter on the horse in a hurry.

Had she had more advance notice she might have considered camouflaging the mottled gray

with hair dye. Sadly, coloring an entire horse was
not a job to be done in haste. Besides, if anybody
saw her with Moonlight the coat color wouldn't
matter as much as the mare's attitude. She dearly
loved Katerina. And the feeling was mutual.

She spoke softly, cajoling as she entered the
stall and displayed the blue halter. "Here you go,
baby. That's a good girl."

Moonlight's upper lip quivered. Her nostrils
flared. Then, to Katerina's astonishment, she
tossed her head and snorted.

"You are so spoiled," Katerina said, reaching
to stroke the silky neck beneath the mane. "Come
on. Be a good girl for me. I'm not going to hurt
you but I am in a hurry."

That was the problem, she realized with a start.
The sensitive animal was picking up on her ner-
vousness and it had caused a negative reaction.
She paused and breathed deeply again in another
attempt to calm herself, as well as the mare, before trying again.

Although the horse did back up a little more
and shuffle her feet in the bedding scattered on
the floor, this time she let herself be haltered. Katerina buckled the chin strap and clipped a lead
rope to the D ring. All the while she kept up the
affectionate banter Moonlight had become accus-
tomed to when they had trained and competed as
a team.

Thick, braided rope in hand, she peeked out of the stall to check the aisle. It was empty except for a couple of the ranch dogs who were going about their usual business, napping, scratching or yawning with boredom.

"A little boredom would be nice right now, wouldn't it, girl?"

Moonlight nickered quietly, blowing hard enough to lift her upper lip and make it quiver.

Katerina shushed her with a hand on her velvety nose. "Easy, girl. That's it. Come on. I need to get you out of here so you're safe."

Where she was going to hide a thousand-pound animal was the biggest conundrum. There wasn't time to hook up a trailer and take her away, even if Katerina still had a pickup truck, and she wasn't about to help herself to one of her father's transport vehicles because she had no desire to be arrested for auto theft. A bareback ride might be the best answer once they reached a place where she could stand higher to pull herself onto the horse's back.

An uneven cadence of the hooves hitting the packed dirt got her attention. "Whoa." Katerina stared at all four legs. Hocks and pasterns looked good. Nothing seemed swollen. Still, *something* was wrong.

With her back to Moonlight's head, she bent and tried to lift a foreleg. "Foot." Not only did the mare resist, she tossed her head and began to fight the halter.

Katerina stopped. If Moonlight jerked the rope out of her hand and escaped there would be no way to make sure she was out of harm's way. Her grip tightened. She cast around, knowing what she should do yet reluctant to rethink her escape plans. Time was passing faster than a fractious colt who had thrown his rider.

"Okay, back to your stall so I can use both hands to figure out what's wrong with you," Katerina told the nervous animal. "I don't want to ruin you for life by making you run."

She grabbed a metal hoof pick that hung on a nail, pocketed it and retraced their path. Hands shaking, she checked her cell phone for the time. She could probably count on about an hour before Max and the other lawmen arrived. That would be enough time to figure out what was wrong with her horse. It would have to be.

Katerina's heart went out to the mare. Heath McCabe was supposed to make sure all the horses were groomed regularly, including having their feet cleaned. He'd been taking Moonlight in for a vet check the day the other barn had exploded. How could this problem have shown up so quickly or been missed in the past?

"Well, whatever's ailing you, I'll fix it, baby," she promised Moonlight. Drawing a hand along the horse's side and giving its rump a pat she urged it back into its stall and shut the bottom half of the door so she could work without an assistant. There weren't many show horses Katerina trusted enough to doctor them alone. This one was the exception.

Bending again, she asked Moonlight to raise one foot. The horse shifted her weight. "That's it, girl. That's what I want."

She was reaching for the hoof pick when one of the ranch dogs started barking. The whole pack immediately joined in.

Katerina froze. It was too early for Kyle. Max might be here already but if so, why were the dogs barking when they had gotten to know him? Her heart thudded painfully in her chest.

Without rising, she released her hold on the mare's foreleg and crouched in the stall. The barking was getting worse. Closer. And she was trapped with the very animal she'd come there to rescue.

Max had stationed himself in the hotel lobby to wait for his backup early so he'd be certain Katerina was behaving herself upstairs.

Maybe he shouldn't have kissed her at all, but his raw emotions had finally won that battle. What he was or wasn't going to do about it later was a whole other dilemma. The way he figured, one catastrophe at a time. Maybe, once she felt safe and stopped feeling like a victim, she wouldn't be interested in a romance with him at all.

"Well, that's a depressing thought," he grumbled to himself as several black-and-white patrol cars pulled up in front. Max could see that some hotel guests were uneasy about such a strong police presence so he went to meet the others in the driveway. Opal was by his side.

"My dog's coming in case we need her," Max announced. "May as well be covered."

"Three units of city police went on ahead," the closest deputy informed him. "Our boss went with them to make sure they don't act like old-time cowboys on a Saturday night spree and shoot up the place."

"Sounds good to me." He'd started for his SUV when the deputy leaned out the window of his cruiser and called, "What happened to your pretty sidekick?"

"She's right here," Max said, indicating Opal and pretending he didn't know who the man was asking about.

"Right," someone else drawled. "Personally, I like the ones that look like Ms. Katerina. Thought you did, too."

"I have a job to do. We all do," Max said tersely. "Let's get a move on."

He huffed as he climbed into his SUV. So, his

personal feelings were that obvious. Big surprise. It seemed that he and Katerina were the only ones missing the signals. Had she been sending them to him? Undoubtedly. He even recalled rebuffing her at least once when she'd tried to hug him. That kind of casual exchange of affection had begun as no more than the innocent moral support of one human being for another. When had it changed, grown into something so much more? Perhaps the metamorphosis had been so subtle that neither of them had noticed. Or maybe they had both been denying their mutual attraction for different reasons.

Joining the convoy bound for the Garwood ranch, Max had plenty of time to mull over his feelings for Katerina. He had admired her from the moment when she'd tried to ignore her own injuries to go check on the welfare of animals. She'd have done it, too, if he had not forced her to accept medical attention. That kind of self-sacrificing attitude was commendable as long as it didn't get her hurt.

Somehow, after that, he'd started to take a personal interest in her welfare. He hadn't purposely decided to do so, it had simply happened, which was the main reason he'd ordered her to stay in her hotel room. Yes, she was mad at him. And yes, she might hold a grudge. But he'd had to do it. As long as his attention was divided, his success was in jeopardy. More than one agent had ended a promising career that way—and not necessarily by retiring at a ripe old age.

Max instinctively knew he'd be willing to sacrifice himself for Katerina, he just didn't want to. Not if he could look forward to spending the rest of his life with her.

That conclusion hit him hard. There was the key to settling all their manageable conflicts. At least he hoped so. If he confessed his love and she didn't reciprocate, he didn't know how he'd take it. She had to care for him. She had to. And it had to be love, not anything else, such as a desire to escape her critical parent or leave a town that had turned against her.

He began to smile as the convoy neared the Garwood Ranch. After he'd bared his heart he planned to tell her all about his ranch in Montana. She'd love it there. It wasn't a big spread but it was all his, his and his brothers'. There was plenty of room for another house, too, if it came to that.

But for right now… Max slowed and parked out of sight in a grove of trees while the sheriff's men spread out and found their own places to hide.

Since he and Katerina had been seen together so often he hoped the sight of him, if he were spotted, would not put Kyle off and endanger the horses or Garwood. Of all the lawmen present, he was the most easily identifiable, the only one working a dog.

He led the boxer up the driveway, keeping to the edges in case they were being watched. The first long, rectangular block of stalls was occupied by horses, he knew, but Opal's body language did not yet indicate the presence of strangers. Not that he was positive she was reliable in that capacity. All he had to go by was the instinct she'd displayed after the parade.

Max's jaw clenched and a shiver shot up his spine. Of all the actions he'd taken since arriving in South Fork, the smartest had to be his decision to insist that Katerina stay out of this final showdown.

There was a good chance someone would die today.

He didn't want it to be her.

Crouching out of sight and trusting Moonlight to avoid stepping on her, Katerina listened, hoping to pick up clues to who was nearby. The barking of the ranch dogs kept her from hearing clearly but she knew they wouldn't bother raising a fuss over any of the regular employees. Therefore, either the police were already here or Kyle had outsmarted them all.

"Please, Father," she whispered, "make it one of the good guys."

Her arms and legs felt as weak as if she'd just run miles. She was weaponless. Hemmed in. And as useless as a saddle without a horse.

"Lord, I'm sorry," she said, her lips barely moving. Unshed tears blurred her vision as she thought of the man she loved and added, "I'm so sorry, Max."

Moonlight's ears swiveled forward. Her deep brown eyes widened until Katerina could see white rims around the pupils. The horse was getting frightened. And, as a result of animal's signals, so was Katerina.

She duckwalked over to the front wall of the stall and pressed an ear to the wood. Men were talking. If only those dogs would shut up she might be able to figure out who it was and what was being said.

A deep voice shouted. Something metallic crashed against the wall. A bucket had been thrown, probably at the pack of excited dogs, because their barking quieted.

"You stay here and mind the horse while I go take care of Garwood," one of the men said.

Breathless, Katerina heard a muted rebuttal. "What about the other? You know."

"Taken care of. One push of a button."

"I don't like that idea." The voice was gravely, as if the speaker was nursing a sore throat.

"Too bad. I'm the one with the gun so that

makes me boss. Now do as you're told or you'll get the first bullet instead of the old man."

Dad! Katerina's emotions churned. She felt ill. *Why didn't I start with the house?* One glance at the horse towering over her and she knew she had chosen wisely. If she had stayed her course, at least one of the threats against those she loved would have been thwarted.

It was suddenly easy to identify with Max and see why he blamed himself for prior mistakes in judgment. She'd had more than one choice this morning and had taken the wrong path. Her motives had been good but her conduct was not nearly as honorable as it should have been. She had let a lie of omission stop her from making wise decisions. False pride had brought her here.

Katerina bit her lip to keep from weeping. She wasn't nearly as clever as she'd thought she was and it was almost time to pay a high price for her inflated opinion of herself.

As she sagged against the front wall of the stall, the exposed end of the metal hoof pick in her back pocket bumped against the wood. A tapping sound that would normally have been almost inaudible seemed to echo like the thrown bucket had.

She held her breath. Froze. Prayed silently that whoever was in the aisle had not noticed. If he came any closer and looked down he might be able to see her despite the barred top half of the wall.

Seconds dragged by. Katerina didn't move. Maybe she was safe. Maybe she'd gotten away with accidentally making the tiny noise.

Then, her dapple gray mare started to move. Careful to avoid stepping on Katerina she ambled to the open half door and put her head through the opening as she always did when greeting friends or begging for treats.

Shadows above told the story. A man was coming closer, reaching out, stroking the horse's forehead and scratching between her ears.

Moonlight knows him! Katerina realized. And suddenly she did, too. The shirtsleeve was familiar. So was the crooning tone he was now using. One of her enemies was Heath McCabe!

As soon as he realized Moonlight should not be wearing a halter, he'd know exactly who had put it on her and would start searching.

The game was over. She'd lost.

EIGHTEEN

Max spotted Kyle in the distance. He was about to follow when Opal began to pull him in a different direction. The radio earpiece kept incoming transmissions muted so he called in his location and reported the situation.

"We have men coming up on the back of the ranch house now. Hold your position," was the reply.

He didn't intend to argue command hierarchy, particularly not when Opal was so intent on leading him to the barns. Whatever the dog wanted at this point was fine with Max. If she happened to turn up another bomb, so be it. If not, he could work his way into position to intercept Kyle if and when he headed back that way.

They rounded the first rectangular barn. Opal began straining at the leash and wagging her stub of a tail along with the rest of her rear half.

For the briefest of moments, Max was so thunderstruck he couldn't make himself believe his eyes. His jaw dropped open. "No. No, no, no."

"You okay, Agent West?" This time it was Sheriff Tate, himself, who was asking.

"No. Have somebody bring my car to me. Park it in plain view."

"Keys?"

Max recited the code for the locked door. "Keys are in the ignition."

"You sure? I thought we'd agreed to do this covertly."

"That was before I saw this." Max snapped a quick photo of Katerina's rented car and sent it to the sheriff.

The older man's reaction was as expected. He cursed. "I thought you were sure that young woman wasn't mixed up in all of this. If she's innocent, why did she come to warn her buddies?"

"They aren't her friends," Max insisted, keeping his voice down and letting Opal approach to sniff the green car. "If anything, Katerina's in deep trouble already. That's why I want my car brought up. We were sneaking around to protect her. Since she's already here I want her to know that I am, too."

"Okay, if you say so. Just remember, this is your party, not mine."

That verbal transfer of authority and therefore blame, struck Max as ironic. Truth to tell, he didn't care who was in charge. All he cared about was finding Katerina and spiriting her out of harm's way. Later, when he had her alone and could express himself without having it broadcast all over the county, he intended to have words with her. And unless he managed to calm down before then, they were probably going to be very harsh words.

Providing she's all right, he added silently. If something happened to steal her from him the way his first fiancée had been taken years before, he didn't know if his heart—or his mind— would survive.

Terror filled Katerina. Moonlight sensed her distress and shied away from the ranch foreman, her ears laid back and her eyes once again wild-looking. That helped expose Katerina's hiding place. There wasn't a thing she could do about it except remain very still, hold her breath and mentally call out to God. It wasn't the way she'd been taught to pray by her late mother but at the moment it was the best she could do. At least she was already on her knees.

The noisy rumble of a diesel engine drifted to her. There were several trucks on the ranch that ran on diesel fuel but that one sounded more powerful. Like Max's SUV!

Confirmation came from McCabe. "Well, well, well. Look who's here. Mr. FBI himself."

To her relief, the foreman stepped away from the stall. She stretched her cramped legs by pulling herself up and peeking through the bars. When Moonlight came up behind her and breathed down her neck she reached around and gave the mare a pat.

There had to be something close by she could use to defend herself until help arrived. But what? The hooked end of the hoof pick in her pocket was blunted to keep from hurting the tender center of a horse's hoof called the frog, so it was useless for self-defense.

A pitchfork might work. If there was one around. Given her father's strict rules about keeping a tidy barn she doubted it.

"Keep going," she whispered, watching McCabe cautiously working his way down the aisle to the far door. If he left the barn she might get a chance to make a run for it. And if she reached her car and made a lot of noise driving away, Heath and the man she assumed was Kyle might give chase.

Someone shouted. Katerina ducked down, holding her shaky breath and clenching her fists. Another man yelled, his words so faint she figured he had to be much farther away.

"Far is good," she muttered. "Just give me a little distance. That's all I ask."

Braced with her hand on the latch to the stall door, she waited and listened. Her fingers tightened. The horse behind her whinnied softly, as if joining in the moment of decision. Almost time. Almost time…

A bang cracked the still air like a hammer breaking a brittle rock.

Katerina fell back, shocked speechless. Horses panicked, kicking at their stalls and calling to each other. That was a gunshot. She knew it was. And since it had rattled every fiber of her being, she knew it had originated in the barn.

Max's name was in her heart and almost on her lips. If they had hurt him she was going to attack them with her bare hands. Pound them with her fists. She was…

Reality overwhelmed her and sapped her strength. She wasn't going to do a thing. She had behaved as if she belonged in a bad movie and had walked into this mess with her eyes open. Now she was going to have to face her fate the same way, like it or not.

Standing tall, she dashed away tears. The air was still, the atmosphere fraught with anxiety. Moonlight was almost as upset as the other horses so she offered comfort, wondering if this was the last time she'd have an opportunity to show love to the magnificent animal.

"Easy, girl. Easy." Katerina began with soft, calming strokes, then laid her cheek against the horse's sleek neck and hugged her, weeping, the way she had so many times in the past. They had shared a lot of good days, a lot of wonderful memories. Her only regret was that those days were probably about to come to an abrupt end.

Thoughts of mounting bareback and charging out of the barn in a daring escape flitted through Katerina's mind. Moonlight might survive that way even if she didn't. Then again, knowing how horses behaved, she knew it wouldn't be long until memories of a cozy stall and plenty of alfalfa hay drew her back home. Then what would become of her with no protector, especially if McCabe chose to take his frustration out on the helpless mare?

As the horse quieted, it became clear that a race to safety was totally out of the question. Shuffling around in fright had noticeably worsened the mare's sore foot. She came to a stop with one foreleg resting on the leading edge of that hoof, as though she were a ballerina on point.

Katerina gave the aisle a quick glance, saw that it was empty and took out the hoof pick. This might be her last chance to minister to her sweet companion and she wasn't going to waste it.

Tears clouded her vision and dripped onto the

underside of the hoof as she cleaned it out. There was a big rock wedged between the tender frog and the inside edge of the shoe. No wonder poor Moonlight was limping.

Katerina dashed away her tears, sniffled and persisted. McCabe and his buddy were probably going to shoot her anyway so she was going to give him a piece of her mind. Leaving an obstruction like this was shameful.

Raking at the rock she cleared away everything else that was packed around it. The gray color reminded her of Half Dome in Yosemite Park. The shape, however was odd.

Suddenly it all came to her. Vern had hung around the stables a lot. She'd thought he was there to keep her company but maybe he'd had ulterior motives. If Heath had been telling the truth about taking horses to the vet, this clump of material would have been discovered already. Since it was still here, there was a good chance he'd lied and was merely clearing out the barn before the planned destruction.

Did that mean he hadn't known about the diamonds at that time? It must, because, as Max had speculated, he had blown up a place where they may have been hidden.

So where did Kyle come in? Had he and Vern really been close friends? Or had he been sent by a higher-up to retrieve Vern's stash?

Finally, Katerina got the nose of the pick under an edge of the gray glob and heard it pop loose. The noise startled Moonlight.

Was this what everybody had been looking for? Almost afraid to find out she was wrong, Katerina slowly reached beneath the horse's belly and fisted the object. On the bottom, where it had met the hoof and been protected, she could see sparkling beneath a sheet of clear plastic. This was it! She'd found the hidden treasure!

Before she could straighten she heard a masculine hoot of triumph behind her.

They knew.

Max had heard a shot, seen it shatter the windshield in his SUV and had checked with Sheriff Tate to make sure nobody was injured.

"My deputy bailed out on the passenger side and made a run for it," was the reply. "He's fine. Sorry about the car."

"It's replaceable. People aren't. Don't worry."

"What now?"

"I'm behind the first barn with Katerina's car. I don't see her yet. Opal and I are going to check the next one. I think that's where the shot came from."

"Affirmative. Be advised. Bertrand Garwood is there, too. One of the guys we're after just brought him out of the house and perp-walked him your direction."

"Copy." Max gritted his teeth. It was becoming more a question of who *wasn't* there than who was. The only thing more ironic would be the addition of drug lord Angus Dupree, missing agent Jake Morrow and maybe runaway witness Esme Dupree. That would make the roster just about complete.

Of course, not being absolutely positive which side Jake was on these days might complicate matters. So did having Katerina's father on scene. Max was pretty sure Garwood was innocent but that didn't guarantee his safety. Nothing could. When Kyle found out that Vern's secret had died with him, bullets were likely to start flying. At this point, Max wasn't sure whether he was angry at Katerina or merely petrified of losing her.

Pulling Opal to heel on a tight leash, he drew his sidearm and began to edge forward.

Someone began to cheer and whoop it up.

Max's gut twisted. He picked up the pace. Reached the rear barn door.

And saw two men slapping each other on the back while Bertrand stood by and stared.

Three accounted for. Why were they so ecstatic? And where was Katerina?

Standing between the threat and Moonlight, Katerina let Kyle and Heath celebrate all they wanted. She didn't care one whit about hidden diamonds. All she cared about was Max, her beloved horse—and her father.

In that order? she asked herself, answering *yes* with the addition of her heavenly Father as number one. The way she saw the future, her fate could tip either way and the longer her enemies gloated, the better for all concerned.

From her position inside the stall she couldn't see much beyond her father. Hoping for at least a modicum of moral support, she caught Bertrand's attention and tried to smile before mouthing, "I love you."

His response was chilling. "This is all your fault, Katerina. I hope you're happy. Why didn't you put an end to it before it escalated and turn over the diamonds?"

"Because I didn't know where they were."

"Bah. You expect me to believe that?"

She stood tall. "I don't care if you do or not. If any of you do. The only reason I discovered Vern's hiding place is because Moonlight was limping."

Kyle punched Heath in the shoulder. Hard. "Amateurs! I told you it was a mistake to just take those horses for a ride and bring them straight back. You should of had them vet-checked like you said you were going to."

"Yeah, well, if you'd gotten closer to Vern before he was arrested we wouldn't be standin' here at all."

"I wasn't sent here in time." Fists raised, Kyle squared off on Heath. "You brought the feds. You and that dumb idea to teach your boss a lesson by setting off a little explosion. Some little explosion. The whole barn went."

"Only because it caught fire. Besides, you were keeping the diamonds a secret back when I did that. How was I supposed to know it was a stupid idea?"

"If you had a brain under that cowboy hat you'd have figured it out for yourself."

"Fine." Heath backed down and glanced toward the open stall. "What're we gonna do now?"

"Clean up this mess."

"How? We can't just shoot 'em."

"Maybe you can't, but I can."

The ranch manager held up his hands. "Hold on. I didn't sign up for murder. Vern gettin' killed in jail is one thing. This ain't the same. Not a bit."

Katerina saw Kyle's expression harden, his eyes narrowing. "You have no idea who I am, do you?"

When Heath didn't reply Katerina wanted to jump in and ask for her own sake. Kyle had led her to believe they had met months ago. Now she doubted whether or not that was true. He'd spoken and acted like a local good ol' boy before. Now he sounded totally different and far too intelligent. She studied the man, waiting, wondering.

Bertrand Garwood cursed, directing most of

his tirade toward Kyle, and Katerina realized immediately that it was a big mistake. She edged backward until her shoulders touched Moonlight's. She and the horse weren't the only ones nervous enough to tremble. Heath was doing a perfect impression of a sapling being buffeted by Santa Ana winds and it served him right. Only her father acted clueless, perhaps because he hadn't realized how deep a pile of manure he was figuratively standing in. "He's saying he's a gangster, Dad. I'd cool it if I were you."

"Don't be ridiculous. This isn't the 1940s or '50s. That era is long gone."

"Correct," Kyle said with a leering smile. "I work for businessmen. That's all they do. Business. We have connections all over the world and once in a while one of our deliveries goes missing. That's where I come in. I see that justice is done." He laughed. "I just do it my way."

"Dupree," Katerina whispered before realizing she'd said it aloud.

Kyle turned on her. "Smart. I knew you were. That's too bad."

She raised her hands, palms forward, to fend him off. "Go. Take the diamonds, all of them. We won't say a word, will we?"

Her eyes pled with the other two men, each in turn. Heath seemed ready to cave but Bertrand was his usual bombastic self. "After all you've done? All you and your kind have cost me? Not on your life."

"How about on *your* life?" Kyle drawled.

The older man blustered. "Do you know who I am? I'm the mayor of South Fork. Sheriff Tate is a personal friend of mine."

"Then you'll have plenty of mourners at your funeral, Mr. Mayor." Waving the pistol, Kyle used it to point at the stall where Katerina and Moonlight stood. "Everybody in. Now. I want to do this right to impress the feds and I haven't got all day."

Nobody moved.

All Katerina could think of was Max, praying he hadn't been shot. When he hadn't returned fire she'd feared the worst, yet held on to the hope that he'd chosen to merely take cover, not suspecting that she or anyone else was in jeopardy.

That had to be it. He could not be gone forever. They had to meet again, if only long enough for her to tell him how much she loved him.

NINETEEN

Max overheard everything. It was all he could do to hold himself back. He'd advised Tate of the situation and was waiting until more officers were in position before giving the order to storm the barn.

His elite team would have had a better chance of success. Trouble was, they weren't there. He was essentially on his own. And he didn't like it. Superheroes were a fantasy. Real men, real agents, used their brains and technology to outwit criminals, they didn't go charging into danger dodging a hail of bullets.

Or running through a minefield, he added. It was time to activate some of their usual precautions. He turned his back on the open door, hunched over his cell phone and called Dylan O'Leary.

"What's up," the tech guru said. "I see it's you but I can hardly hear your voice, Max."

He cupped the small device and tried again. "Can you kill all cell signals from the relay towers around my location?" In the background he could hear computer keys clacking.

"I can, but you'll lose the ability to talk to me."

"We can communicate by police radio, relaying via a landline at their station, if we have to."

"Do we have time to ask for permission?"

"No."

"That's what I figured. Can you at least fill me in so I'm prepared when they threaten to fire me again?"

"A Dupree hitman is holding people at gunpoint and I can't figure out why he hasn't shot them yet. If he's the same one who's been planting bombs around here, he may not need to. The place may already be wired."

"Copy. Works for me. How long do I have?"

"Time is already up," Max said. "Just do your best."

Katerina was out of ideas. Apparently her father was, too. Kyle gave him a hard push and he ended up inside the stall.

"You, too," the Dupree cohort said to Heath.

"Hey, wait a minute, man. You and I are in this together."

"Right. Do you really think I'd join forces with the likes of you? I needed help on the inside, that's all. I don't need you anymore." He motioned with the gun barrel again. "Move it."

If Katerina had not been so disappointed in the foreman she might have felt sorrier for him. As it was, she could hardly bear to be near him.

"You were like an uncle to me," she rasped. "How *could* you?"

"It was comin' to me. I ain't had a raise in five years. A man's gotta eat."

Bertrand interrupted. "There was nothing coming to you that you deserved."

Shocked, Katerina turned on her father. "This is partly your fault, after all. When are you going to learn to treat everybody fairly?"

The stall door started to swing closed with the gunman on the outside. "Don't hold your breath, lady," he taunted. "There won't be time for any of you to reform."

Pleading and weeping openly, McCabe dropped to his knees in what was left of the opening. That was enough distraction for Katerina to duck, crawl beneath Moonlight's belly and pull out the cell phone Max had given her. The only number entered in it was his so she opted to dial 9-1-1.

What she had not counted on was the loud "Nine-one-one. What is your emergency?" reply.

Kyle shouted obscenities and started shoving the others aside to get to her.

Katerina screamed. Slipped her phone beneath the straw bedding. And heard glass break when Moonlight sidestepped in fright and crushed it.

Bedlam ensued. Katerina rolled aside, hoping to keep from being grabbed or shot. Heath scrambled out the open stall door like the crabs she'd seen crossing hot sand along the Pacific coast, twenty miles due west.

Bertrand Garwood went for the gun and failed. Kyle's punch flattened him.

Breathing hard, the hired thug kept his back to the side wall and the pistol trained on his remaining captives while he pulled out his own cell phone.

"Okay, this is how it's going to be," he said with a sneer before glancing at his revolver. "I like this piece so I was trying to keep from leaving ballistics but sometimes you have to make sacrifices. I can always pick up another one like it on the street."

He cocked the hammer with his thumb. "I'll do the horse first so it doesn't get in my way again."

"No!" Katerina launched herself at him.

Moonlight reared. Her hooves grazed Kyle's arm and deflected the bullet he fired as a reflex.

Katerina shrieked. Was she hit? Was her mare? Was her father?

The pistol barrel came up again, pointed right at Moonlight. Screaming unintelligibly, Katerina lurched toward it.

Instead of firing this time, Kyle used it to bat her away, the blow propelling her across the stall where she slammed into a solid plank wall. Reality dimmed. She began to feel as if she were floating above the conflict, a feather in the wind.

Another shot echoed. Katerina was too groggy to react. Sliding to the straw in a heap she closed her eyes and passed out.

Max was running full out. So was Opal. He'd heard the loud response from the emergency operator and had anticipated a negative result. Boy, had he been right.

Plastering himself against the outer wall of the stall where the battle was taking place, he commanded Opal and the gathering lawmen to wait while he made a silent entry. Sweat dotted his forehead, His hands were slippery. He wiped them dry on his jeans and braced for counterattack, then whipped around the corner and came face-to-face with the armed criminal.

Instead of firing, Max hesitated. This man had admitted working for the Duprees. His insider knowledge might be invaluable—if he could bring him in alive.

"Drop the gun."

"Sure." He tossed it aside.

That didn't fit the profile. What was Max missing? He didn't dare take his focus off Kyle to check the Garwoods. Both were down and out, although neither showed signs of serious injury.

It took Max only a few heartbeats to deduce the problem. Kyle no longer needed his gun because he had another weapon in hand. His cell phone. He was holding it in front of him, pointing it like a laser. There was only one logical conclusion. He was preparing to detonate more bombs. On the ranch. And these weren't like Heath's meager efforts. These were seriously deadly.

"Don't," Max warned, eyeing the phone.

"Then get out of my way and let me go."

Had Dylan succeeded in cutting off the cell signals? Katerina had gotten through to 9-1-1 so if he had managed to kill the phones it had happened within the last couple of minutes. Max couldn't take the chance. He retreated in the direction of Katerina's still form, although he didn't turn his back on the hired killer.

Katerina began to stir. Blinked and looked up at him. "Max. You're alive."

"Yes." There was nothing more he could do to prevent the planted bombs from exploding. If this was his final second on earth he was exactly where he needed to be. With his woman. Best of all, she was smiling up at him, He knelt to cradle her head and shoulders.

"I need to tell you," she began.

"Hush, honey. Everything's fine. I've got you."

There was no way for him to tell if his back and

vest would shield her enough to keep her alive during an explosion but he intended to try.

She slipped one arm around his neck. "I have to say it. I love you, Max."

"I love you, too."

Pulling her closer he gave Kyle a sidelong glance and saw his evil grin as he dramatically pushed one of the buttons on the phone he held.

Nothing happened!

Max wanted to cheer.

Katerina was so focused on being back in Max's strong arms she was late noticing how intently he was watching Kyle. When she saw the criminal's sinister expression and the way he was handling his phone, she realized what was going on.

"Freeze," Max shouted. "Hands on your head."

Instead, Kyle threw the phone, pulled a second gun from a holster strapped to his ankle and ran.

"Get him!" Katerina screeched.

"Are you…?"

"Fine. *Stop* him. He works for the Dupree crime family."

"I know. See to your dad."

Katerina had no trouble doing that. Bertrand was very subdued, sitting on the floor and holding his head. "Dad?"

"He shot me!"

"Apparently." She gently pulled his hand away from his forehead. "It's just a scratch. Your hard head must have deflected the bullet."

The confused look he gave her wasn't conciliatory but it wasn't angry, either. Maybe there was hope for them, at least to the point where they stopped being avowed enemies.

"Are you okay?" Bertrand asked hoarsely. "I saw him pitch you across the stall."

"Guess I have a hard head, too," Katerina said. "It runs in the family."

They paused to exchange quizzical looks just as a volley of shots echoed through the barn.

Katerina gasped. "Max."

Bertrand patted her hand. "He'll be okay. Listen. I can hear him yelling orders."

"You're right." Although she managed a smile, there were tears of gratitude to God in her eyes.

"I sure like this one better than Kowalski."

She sniffled and shook her head. "I'm so used to doing the opposite of whatever you want I hardly know what to say."

"Never mind me. When he asks you, say yes."

"What if he doesn't want to get married?"

"Then you convince him." The older man started to chuckle and winced. "Ouch."

"You'll probably have a dandy headache, Dad."

"Not as bad as the headaches you gave me trying to raise you without a mother. I was scared to death of making a mistake. When you said you wanted to marry that oddball, Kowalski, I figured I'd failed big-time."

"*That*'s what turned you against me? I thought you were ashamed of me."

"I was. And of myself for not being a better father." He started to frown, then moaned and grabbed his forehead again. "I thought, when I said it was him or me, you'd come to your senses."

"And when I didn't, you stuck to your guns."

"Of course I did. What other choice did I have?"

Katerina had absorbed all the regret she could handle so she grabbed Moonlight's lead rope and led the mare out into the wide aisle at the center of the long rectangular barn. Thankfully, the limp was almost gone.

What had happened to the diamonds? Katerina could not have cared less. Wealth was not the answer to happiness. Oh, it could mask deficiencies for a while but in the end, a person needed much more. Like love and companionship. A mare like Moonlight. And, she thought, glancing at the knot of men gathered at the open barn door and spotting the FBI logo on Max's vest, she needed him.

Just then he turned and saw her. His wide grin spoke volumes as he broke away from the group and started to hurry her way. Moonlight whinnied. Katerina dropped the halter rope and rushed toward Max.

They met, arms open for each other, and held tight.

He stroked her back. "It's over, honey. It's all over. As soon as Opal and I clear out any hidden explosives this threat will end."

She desperately wanted his conclusion to prove true. "How can you be sure?"

"Because I'm going to announce finding the diamonds and explain that they have been turned over to the prosecutor as additional evidence of motive in Reginald Dupree's and Kyle's trials. Even if the US Marshals can't find Esme Dupree so we can put her on the witness stand, we'll have a concrete reason why Kowalski was killed."

"And the drug charges?"

"Yes. Those, too."

"Thank the Lord."

"I have been," Max confessed. "You were right about my needing to come back to my faith. I'm real good at telling everybody else to accept the bad with the good. I just wasn't as good at taking my own advice." His smile softened and he tenderly kissed her.

"Which am I?" Katerina asked, hoping with all her heart for a positive answer.

"Good," Max whispered against her lips. "Very good."

Sighing and enjoying their closeness, Katerina tried to wait for what she thought was coming. Three amazing kisses later Max relaxed his hold and started to say, "Well, I guess Opal and I..."

"Hold it, Special Agent West. You've forgotten something."

"I don't think so."

"Yes, you have. Aren't you going to ask me to marry you and go to Montana?"

A stunned look replaced his smile.

"Uh-oh." Katerina felt like weeping. "I was mistaken?"

After seconds that felt like hours to her, Max recovered and quirked a smile. "That might be the only way I can keep you out of trouble." He eyed the open stall. "That was not the smartest move you've ever made."

"I did it for the right reasons, though."

His smile spread. "That's debatable. So, could you ever bring yourself to leave California?"

That was a very positive sign. "Watch how fast I can pack."

"You haven't asked me anything about my plans for the future or where I live or what my job entails. How do you know you'd be happy?"

"I'll be with you. What else matters?"

Judging by the way his shoulders relaxed and his smile returned, this conversation was going to end well.

Gazing deeply into her eyes, Max said, "I have a ranch in Montana. My brothers and I are co-owners but they pretty much let me do my own thing. There's even room for your horse."

"There is?" Squealing with delight she threw her arms around Max's neck. He swung Katerina in a circle and kissed her again.

"Does that mean your answer is *yes*," he teased.

"Well…" Katerina was so happy she was giddy. Bursting into laughter she managed a quick "Yes!"

It didn't surprise Max to see that most of the remaining law officers were grinning at him and Katerina. If he'd witnessed their interchange he would have been, too. As it was, he had trouble wiping the smile off his face long enough to do a thorough search of the Garwood Ranch.

An encounter with Bertrand as paramedics treated his superficial wound gave him a chance to ask about buying Katerina's horse.

"No need," the older man said. "It's hers. I heard you two talking in the barn. She can take the mare and I'll throw in a new truck and trailer for the trip."

"Really?"

Garwood nodded. "Yes. She earned it with all the work she did around here as a teenager. I paid her entry fees and outfitted her and the horse, but she never got wages the way the other trainers did.

It's recently been pointed out to me that I wasn't a fair boss."

"It's true that your foreman set the first bomb here. We found components in his pickup."

"Ah, so that's why his room was so clean. I wondered."

"He'll have to be tried."

"I'll think about getting him a lawyer. We do go way back." He winced. "Ouch."

The paramedic merely smiled as if enjoying doctoring the usually pompous mayor.

"Have you been over the whole ranch yet?"

"Yes," Max said. "Opal and I located three sets. If Kyle had been able to get a cell signal when he tried, there wouldn't be much left of this place but it's safe now." Looking around and taking in the bucolic setting, Max added, "Have you seen Katerina?"

"Yeah. She's in the barn where we had all the fun. I saw her go in there with one of the farm dogs."

"Thanks."

"You treat her good, you hear."

Max saluted casually. "It will be my pleasure." In retrospect he wasn't totally sure how he'd gotten himself engaged so fast but he wasn't going to complain. They didn't have to rush into a wedding although he had no qualms about doing it. Katerina was perfect for him. He'd known that from their first meeting and had not changed his mind since.

He went straight to the barn and began searching stalls. If not for Opal he might have missed spotting her in the shadowy rear corner of one unoccupied by a horse. What it did hold, besides the love of his life, was the black lab she had mentioned before. The dog was happily nursing a squirming litter.

"Pups! How many?"

"Five." Katerina smiled up at him.

Max crouched next to her, blocking Opal so she wouldn't bother the new mother. "What's her name?"

"Dad usually called her something else, but to me she's Baby."

"Since she's a lab, her temperament is probably unsuited for attack or protection, but those pups may have what it takes to be trackers. When we finish an assignment, my team always brings back one or more new prospects for the trainers to test. Would you mind if we adopted a couple of these little guys?"

"I think that would be wonderful. I'd already decided to ask Dad to let me take the mama with me."

Chuckling, Max said, "Well, if you're going to ask him, do it while he's in such a good mood."

"What do you mean?"

"I offered to buy your mare for you and your dad told me he was giving her to you. Her and a rig for hauling her. He called it back wages."

Her eyes widened. "You're serious?"

"Totally. Now all we have to do is plan for you to follow me back to Billings."

He saw her sober as she glanced at the puppies and their mother. Although she didn't say so, he figured she was worried about them if she left too soon.

"Why don't we do this?" Max began. "I'll stay here as long as my assignment can be extended. If no more problems surface now that the Dupree hired gun is in jail, I'll arrange to fly back to visit as often as possible until you and these little guys are ready to travel."

"What excuse can you possibly use?"

"The truth should do it. If not, I'll claim I also need to evaluate these pups before I make a final selection."

"Okay, as long as your choice of a wife doesn't change."

"Honey," Max rasped, afraid his emotions would give away how close he was to weeping with joy. "I have never had a woman propose to me before. I wouldn't dare change my mind. You already have me scared silly."

"You? The self-important, special agent in the

protective vest with your calling printed big enough to read from outer space? You? Scared of me?"

Max pulled her gently to her feet and wrapped her in his embrace. "Only of losing you," he whispered against her hair. "I want us to be together for eternity."

"I couldn't agree more," Katerina said softy.

With pups making contented sounds and the two adult dogs panting in the background, Max closed his eyes and kissed the woman who would soon be his bride.

EPILOGUE

Katerina had no doubt Max would keep his word, and he did. They spent many happy hours working with the young lab puppies and he chose two. She adopted the mother dog and couldn't wait to take them all with her to their new home in Montana.

All three canines, plus Opal and several of the other FBI K-9 officers, attended their outdoor nuptials in Yosemite National Park. The weather was perfect and except for a wild whitetail deer who decided to crash the party and nearly created chaos amidst the dogs, the ceremony went off without a hitch.

Afternoon sun reflected off Half Dome. A breeze ruffled Katerina's veil. Wildflowers bloomed in abundance thanks to a few brief showers in weeks prior. And, wonder of wonders, Bertrand Garwood gave the bride away.

Dylan O'Leary was Max's best man. Katerina hardly noticed him as the music began and she started walking toward her destiny. The *best* man in the world was her very own Special Agent Max West.

He beamed the moment he caught sight of her and never took his eyes off her until she stood beside him, holding his hand, and handed her bouquet to maid of honor, Zara Fielding, Dylan's betrothed.

"I can't believe this is happening," Katerina whispered to Max.

"You still want to go through with it so soon?"

"Yes." She smiled behind the thin white veil. "I've dreamed of being married here since I was a little girl. Thank you for agreeing instead of telling me I was being silly the way everybody else did."

Max was grinning. "All right, then. Let's do it."

Max hadn't had to coerce his family members to attend. They were all delighted, not only that he had found someone like Katerina but that they also got to make a vacation out of the trip.

As they posed for professional photos in the shade of a mighty oak, he gave his bride a quick hug. "I told you my family would love you."

"I was less worried about them than I was my own dad. He sounded more mellow right after the barn shooting but I wasn't sure that change would last."

"I know. I had a little talk with him."

Katerina began to giggle.

"What's so funny?"

"I thought the father of the bride was supposed to have that talk with the groom, not the other way around."

Max appreciated her humor. "Ah, but I was already perfect. He was the one who needed an attitude adjustment."

"You're modest, too, I see."

"Absolutely."

Katerina sobered slightly. "I'm sorry your whole unit couldn't be here. Last-minute assignments?"

"Yes. Harper was the most upset to miss seeing us get married. They got another hot tip on Penny Potter and she had to go follow up."

"The brother of the missing agent?"

"Yes. We figured he'd be the most likely to recognize Jake from a distance, in case he's no longer being held captive as some are starting to suggest. Plus, Harper needed the backup."

"Backup? Besides that gorgeous German shepherd I saw in the picture with her? I can't imagine why. He looks ferocious."

Max noticed his bride smiling at the little coal-black pups following their mother and tripping over tufts of soft grass. "Those two sure don't look mean."

"I know," Katerina agreed. "They're adorable. I'll have to really work to keep from spoiling them."

"Our trainers will teach you how."

She sighed and nodded, leaning closer to tuck herself under his arm. "Know what the best part is?"

"No, what?"

"We'll all have homes where we're loved and accepted just as we are." She gazed up at him with love. "Even me."

* * * * *

If you enjoyed SPECIAL AGENT,
look for Cara's story, the next book in the
CLASSIFIED K-9 UNIT series
BOUNTY HUNTER by Lynette Eason.

And don't miss a book in the series:

Dear Reader,

As my pastor is fond of pointing out, the past does not have to dictate our future unless we let it. We can be forgiven and turn the page to a new life in Christ if we will surrender to Him. Yes, there may be lingering consequences, but the Lord will help us deal with those and make something great out of what we've learned from past mistakes.

Katerina was too naive and Max too hardened by life, yet they found a middle ground and allowed themselves to embrace change as well as forgiveness.

Every new day is a gift to you from your Father in Heaven. Don't waste it wishing you could change the past. Look toward the future and trust the Creator.

Blessings,

Valerie Hansen

Get 2 Free Books,
Plus 2 Free Gifts—
just for trying the Reader Service!

Love Inspired®

YES! Please send me 2 FREE Love Inspired® Romance novels and my 2 FREE mystery gifts (gifts are worth about $10 retail). After receiving them, if I don't wish to receive any more books, I can return the shipping statement marked "cancel." If I don't cancel, I will receive 6 brand-new novels every month and be billed just $5.24 for the regular-print edition or $5.74 each for the larger-print edition in the U.S., or $5.74 each for the regular-print edition or $6.24 each for the larger-print edition in Canada. That's a saving of at least 13% off the cover price. It's quite a bargain! Shipping and handling is just 50¢ per book in the U.S. and 75¢ per book in Canada.* I understand that accepting the 2 free books and gifts places me under no obligation to buy anything. I can always return a shipment and cancel at any time. Even if I never buy another book, the 2 free books and gifts are mine to keep forever.

Please check one:
☐ Love Inspired Romance Regular-Print
   (105/305 IDN GLQC)

☐ Love Inspired Romance Larger-Print
   (122/322 IDN GLQD)

Name _____ (PLEASE PRINT)

Address _____ Apt. #

City _____ State/Province _____ Zip/Postal Code

Signature (if under 18, a parent or guardian must sign) _____

Mail to the **Reader Service**:
IN U.S.A.: P.O. Box 1867, Buffalo, NY 14240-1867
IN CANADA: P.O. Box 611, Fort Erie, Ontario L2A 9Z9

Want to try two free books from another line?
Call 1-800-873-8635 today or visit www.ReaderService.com.

*Terms and prices subject to change without notice. Prices do not include applicable taxes. Sales tax applicable in N.Y. Canadian residents will be charged applicable taxes. Offer not valid in Quebec. This offer is limited to one order per household. Books received may not be as shown. Not valid for current subscribers to Love Inspired Romance books. All orders subject to credit approval. Credit or debit balances in a customer's account(s) may be offset by any other outstanding balance owed by or to the customer. Please allow 4 to 6 weeks for delivery. Offer available while quantities last.

Your Privacy—The Reader Service is committed to protecting your privacy. Our Privacy Policy is available online at www.ReaderService.com or upon request from the Reader Service.

We make a portion of our mailing list available to reputable third parties that offer products we believe may interest you. If you prefer that we not exchange your name with third parties, or if you wish to clarify or modify your communication preferences, please visit us at www.ReaderService.com/consumerschoice or write to us at Reader Service Preference Service, P.O. Box 9062, Buffalo, NY 14240-9062. Include your complete name and address.

LI17R

Get 2 Free Books,
Plus 2 Free Gifts—
just for trying the Reader Service!

HARLEQUIN

HEARTWARMING™

YES! Please send me 2 FREE Harlequin® Heartwarming™ Larger-Print novels and my 2 FREE mystery gifts (gifts worth about $10 retail). After receiving them, if I don't wish to receive any more books, I can return the shipping statement marked "cancel." If I don't cancel, I will receive 4 brand-new larger-print novels every month and be billed just $5.49 per book in the U.S. or $6.24 per book in Canada. That's a savings of at least 19% off the cover price. It's quite a bargain! Shipping and handling is just 50¢ per book in the U.S. and 75¢ per book in Canada.* I understand that accepting the 2 free books and gifts places me under no obligation to buy anything. I can always return a shipment and cancel at any time. Even if I never buy another book, the 2 free books and gifts are mine to keep forever.

161/361 IDN GLQL

Name	(PLEASE PRINT)	
Address		Apt. #
City	State/Prov.	Zip/Postal Code

Signature (if under 18, a parent or guardian must sign)

Mail to the **Reader Service:**
IN U.S.A.: P.O. Box 1867, Buffalo, NY 14240-1867
IN CANADA: P.O. Box 611, Fort Erie, Ontario L2A 9Z9

Want to try two free books from another line?
Call 1-800-873-8635 today or visit www.ReaderService.com.

* Terms and prices subject to change without notice. Prices do not include applicable taxes. Sales tax applicable in N.Y. Canadian residents will be charged applicable taxes. Offer not valid in Quebec. This offer is limited to one order per household. Books received may not be as shown. Not valid for current subscribers to Harlequin Heartwarming Larger-Print books. All orders subject to credit approval. Credit or debit balances in a customer's account(s) may be offset by any other outstanding balance owed by or to the customer. Please allow 4 to 6 weeks for delivery. Offer available while quantities last.

Your Privacy—The Reader Service is committed to protecting your privacy. Our Privacy Policy is available online at www.ReaderService.com or upon request from the Reader Service.

We make a portion of our mailing list available to reputable third parties that offer products we believe may interest you. If you prefer that we not exchange your name with third parties, or if you wish to clarify or modify your communication preferences, please visit us at www.ReaderService.com/consumerschoice or write to us at Reader Service Preference Service, P.O. Box 9062, Buffalo, NY 14240-9062. Include your complete name and address.

HW17

READERSERVICE.COM

Manage your account online!

- Review your order history
- Manage your payments
- Update your address

> ### We've designed the Reader Service website just for you.

Enjoy all the features!

- Discover new series available to you, and read excerpts from any series.
- Respond to mailings and special monthly offers.
- Browse the Bonus Bucks catalog and online-only exculsives.
- Share your feedback.

Visit us at:

ReaderService.com

RS16R